ALSO BY

DARCY COATES

The Haunting of Ashburn House
The Haunting of Blackwood House
The House Next Door
Craven Manor
The Haunting of Rookward House
The Carrow Haunt
Hunted
The Folcroft Ghosts
The Haunting of Gillespie House
Dead Lake
Parasite
Quarter to Midnight
Small Horrors

House of Shadows
House of Shadows
House of Secrets

Black Winter
Voices in the Snow
Secrets in the Dark
Whispers in the Mist

DEAD LAKE

DARCY COATES

Poisoned Pen
PRESS

Published by Poisoned Pen Press, an imprint of Sourcebooks
P.O. Box 4410, Naperville, Illinois 60567-4410
(630) 961-3900
sourcebooks.com

Dead Lake was originally self-published in 2015 by Black Owl Books. "Whose Woods These Are," "Mannequin," and "Hitchhiker" were originally self-published in the short-story collection *Quarter to Midnight* in 2015 by Black Owl Books.

Library of Congress Cataloging-in-Publication Data

Names: Coates, Darcy, author.
Title: Dead lake / Darcy Coates.
Description: Naperville : Poisoned Pen Press, [2020]
Identifiers: LCCN 2019059647 | (trade paperback)
Subjects: GSAFD: Suspense fiction.
Classification: LCC PR9619.4.C628 D43 2020 | DDC 823/.92--dc23
LC record available at https://lccn.loc.gov/2019059647

Printed and bound in the United States of America.
VP 13 12 11 10 9 8

CONTENTS

DEAD
LAKE

CHAPTER 1

SAM'S BREATH CAUGHT AS she stepped back from the car, jacket in one hand and a luggage bag in the other, and turned to face the densely wooded hills behind her. The strangest sensation had crawled over her, as if she were being watched.

That was impossible, of course. The lakeside cabin was the farthest from civilization Sam had ever been. Nestled deep in Harob Forest and situated at the edge of a large lake, her uncle's property was a two-hour drive from the nearest town. Her uncle Peter had said hiking paths snaked through the forest but only a couple of them came near his part of the lake, and they weren't used often.

Despite that, Sam couldn't stop herself from running her eyes over the dense pine trees and shrubs that grew along the rocky incline. Only a colony of birds fluttering around a nearby conifer and the steady drone of insects broke the silence.

Sam turned back to the two-story cabin. The sun caught on the rough-hewn wood, making it almost seem to glow. It sat as close to the water as it could without compromising its foundations, and a balcony overlooked the lake. The rocky embankment rising behind it merged directly into the mountains, which grew more than a kilometer into the sky.

Peter had built the cabin nearly a decade before as a hobby to keep himself occupied on the weekends. He was proud of it, and rightfully so; Sam knew Peter made his living as a woodworker, but she hadn't expected him to be so proficient at it. The cabin looked as natural as the rocks, as though it could have sprouted out of the ground fully formed.

Sam shifted the luggage bag to her left hand and approached the front door. Her key fit into the lock and turned easily, and a grin grew across her face as the door creaked open.

The cabin's lower level was a single large room. A fireplace sat to her right; a stack of kindling waited for her near the soot-blackened hole, with a bracket holding aged firewood and an ax beside it. Two stuffed armchairs stood on thick animal furs, facing the fireplace. A polished wood table and chairs sat to Sam's left, near the kitchenette that took up the back part of the room. A stairway above the kitchen led to the upper level.

Sam dropped her bag beside the open door and marveled at how clean the room was. Peter said he visited it at least once a month, and he must have been scrupulous with its maintenance. Sam felt in her jacket pocket for the letter he'd given her then unfolded it to reread the characteristically abrupt chicken-scratch scrawl.

Sammy,

Have fun at the cabin. Don't get eaten by bears.

The lake's good for swimming. There's a canoe in the shed. And dry wood. Light a fire when the sun goes down— it gets cold at night.

There's no electricity or phone reception, so don't get into trouble, but if you do, there's a two-way radio in the kitchen cupboard. I wrote the most important codes beside it.

Don't go on the dock. The wood's rotten. I'll fix it next time I'm up there.

There's food in the cupboards. Eat it. You're too skinny.

Love,

Petey

Smiling fondly, Sam tucked the note back into her pocket. The drive from the city had taken most of the day, and the sun was already edging toward the top of the mountains surrounding the lake. Sam hurried back to her car and began bringing in the rest of her luggage.

An easel, watercolors, oils and acrylics, a large wooden box full of mediums, charcoal and pencils, copious brushes, sketchbooks, and a dozen canvases had filled the trunk and both back seats of the car. Sam brought them inside with significantly more care than she'd shown her travel bag, which held only clothes and towels. She placed most of her equipment on the table then opened the easel in the empty space in the room's corner.

Sam adjusted the angle of the easel so it caught the natural light from the window and set a canvas on it. It looked good there, she thought. *Like an artist's dream retreat. If this doesn't get you back into your groove, nothing will.*

The sky was darkening quickly, and Sam knelt in front of the fireplace. She found matches and clumsily lit the kindling in the grate. She hadn't started a fire since her parents had taken her camping when she was a child. She used up most of the kindling before the blaze was strong enough to catch onto the larger pieces of wood.

Satisfied that her fire wasn't about to die, Sam went to explore the second floor. The steep, narrow staircase turned at the corner of the room and led straight into a bedroom, which, like the ground floor, was open plan. There was something resembling a bathroom at the back wall, with a sink, cupboard, mirror, toilet, and a bathtub—but no shower. The sink and bathtub had plugs, but no taps. On examination, Sam found a pipe coming out of the wall, with a drain and a bucket underneath it, set next to a hand pump. She guessed it was connected to a rainwater tank behind the cabin.

Of course. No electricity and no running water.

That meant she would have to heat the water over the fire if she wanted a warm bath. It wouldn't have bothered Peter. He was a mountain man through and through; he loved hunting, fishing, and woodworking, and he probably relished ice-cold showers too.

A large double bed took up most of the room. It held several

6

layers of thick quilts, topped with animal furs. Sam hesitated, felt the furs gingerly, then folded them up and placed them in the cupboard opposite the bed. Sleeping under the skins of dead animals seemed strangely macabre.

The door leading to the balcony stood to her left. Sam opened it and leaned on the sill to absorb the view. The sun had set behind the mountains, but most of the sky was still a pale blue, with tinges of red showing just above the tops of the trees on the west mountain. The glassy lake, which seemed to stretch on forever, reflected the patchy white clouds. Peter's cabin was set at one of the lake's widest points, but to her right, it narrowed and curved around the sides of the hills that cradled it.

The dock protruded from the shore below the cabin, running twenty meters into the lake. Something large and misshapen sat at its end; Sam squinted in the poor light, trying to make out what it was, then her heart faltered as the shape moved.

It was a man, on his knees, bent over the edge of the dock. His broad shoulders trembled as he stared, fixated on the water below.

CHAPTER 2

SAM'S MOUTH HAD DRIED. She squeezed the balcony's banister so tightly that her knuckles turned white. Her mind, shocked and panicky, struggled to pull information together. *Who is he?* Peter had said there weren't any other houses within walking distance. *Is he a hiker? Why's he on our dock?*

She was suddenly acutely aware of just how remote the cabin was. If she went missing, no one would know until she failed to return home a week later. The police would take hours to reach her, even if she could call them, which she couldn't. Any defense would have to come from her own hands.

The man wasn't moving, except for his shoulders, which twitched sporadically. Sam backed away from the balcony, barely daring to breathe, keeping her eyes fixed on the man until he disappeared from sight, then she turned and ran down the cabin's stairs.

I need a weapon—something to intimidate him with or use in self-defense. Sam wrenched open the kitchen drawers, searching for a knife, but she came up with only two small blades that were useless for anything more than chopping carrots. She turned to look around the room, bouncing with anxious energy, and a glint of silver beside the fireplace caught her eye. *The ax. Yes, that'll do nicely.*

Sam gripped its wooden handle and raised it to head height. She gave it an experimental swing and staggered as its weight threw her off-balance. Anxious sweat built over her back and palms as she turned toward the door and licked her lips.

He's probably just a hiker who's gone off the path to have a closer look at the lake.

He was trespassing, though, on what was clearly private property. Worse, he had to know someone was staying there—the car parked out front and the fireplace's glow leaking through the windows were impossible to ignore.

The doorknob felt unusually cold under Sam's fingers. She took a breath to brace herself then shoved the door open and staggered outside, her shaking hands squeezing the ax's handle so tightly that they ached.

Be strong. Be intimidating. Show him that he doesn't want to mess with you.

"Hey, punk, this is private property," she yelled, hoping he wouldn't hear the frightened squeak in her voice. No answer came. Sam squinted at the dock, which was becoming increasingly hard to see in the rapidly failing light. It was empty.

Sam swiveled to look down the length of the shore then turned toward the straggly edges of the forest. The thick shadows created a kaleidoscope of light and darkness. She couldn't see him, but that didn't mean he was gone.

"Did you hear me?" she called, louder this time. "I have a gun and a career in karate."

Complete hyperbole, of course. As a child, she'd had all of two karate lessons before she dropped it in favor of painting classes. The intruder didn't need to know that, though.

Sam listened hard, straining to hear the telltale crunch of footsteps on dry leaves, but, though the woods hummed with the sounds of birds settling down for the night, she couldn't hear any man-made noises. She turned in a complete circle before letting the ax drop to her side, then she returned to the safety of the cabin.

That should have been enough to scare him off, anyway.

Sam took one last look at the lakeshore and the dock then closed the door with a quiet click. The fire had grown nicely, but it had consumed most of the wood, so she dropped the ax back against the wall and knelt to shove fresh logs onto the crackling flames.

The appearance of a stranger in the one place that was supposed to guarantee solitude had shaken her. For all she knew, he could be the only other human for kilometers, and she had no idea who he was or why he'd specifically come to her cabin—or, for that matter, what fascinated him so much about the water at the end of the dock.

Sam rubbed her hands across her face and stood. Worrying wouldn't help her; the man was probably embarrassed at being seen and was already halfway back to his trail. She wouldn't let the fright ruin her first night at the cabin.

As Peter had promised, the kitchen held a large collection of canned foods. Sam sorted through them, wrinkling her nose at the twelve cases of Spam before picking out a can of chicken soup. She found a set of pans hanging beside the sink, and spoons in one of the drawers. Unable to find a can opener, Sam eventually resorted to using one of the small knives to cut a hole in the top of the can to shake the soup through.

She settled back in front of the fire, using thick oven mitts to shield her hands as she held the pot over the flames. Night had well and truly fallen, and the birds were finally silent, giving way to the bats, owls, and other animals of the night. Their calls, alien and jarring, echoed through the woods behind the cabin. The fire was her only source of light, and when the soup was warm enough, she snuggled into one of the armchairs to watch the mesmerizing flames while she ate.

The quiet crackle and pop of the fire, the warm soup, and the plush chair conspired to lull her into a comfortable daze, and she didn't even realize she was falling asleep until the spoon fell out of her hand and hit the floor with a loud *ping*.

"Jeez, Sam, wake up," she mumbled to herself, and stretched out of the chair. She took the pot and spoon to the sink and, after a moment's confusion, figured out how to get a burst of water from the hand pump. She rinsed her utensils, set them to drain, threw the empty can into a large garbage bag, then turned to the canvas in the corner of the room.

Tiredness weighed down her limbs, but the week was supposed to be a chance for her to focus on her art, and she wanted to start it on the right foot. The canvas, one of the larger ones in her collection, seemed horribly imposing. She squinted at it, stupidly hopeful that inspiration would appear before her eyes, but all she could think about was how close the exhibition's deadline was and how pulling out a week before the showing would kill her career before it even started.

The more she thought about the deadline, the harder it was to come up with ideas. She turned away from the canvas, blocking the intimidatingly empty rectangle from her sight, and riffled through the cluttered table until she found her sketchbook.

It had been eight months since she'd last drawn in it, and flipping through the pages was like reliving half-forgotten dreams. There were pages full of hand practice—where she'd agonized over getting the knuckles, fingernails, and veins *just right*—then the page full of water textures and lily pads, followed with a pencil drawing of a curious lizard who'd sat outside her window.

She recognized the point where she'd received the invitation to show her work in the prestigious Heritage Gallery; the pages were suddenly saturated with colors, and the pencil lines became a little too wild to convey their shapes properly. Then there were pages and pages of ideas for her showing. Sam flipped to the last page she'd drawn in, which was full of eyes. That was what she'd almost chosen for her gallery: an array of oils featuring eyes gazing out of teacups, eyes blended into nature, eyes appearing in the cracks of sandstone chimneys…

There was one incredibly familiar pair of eyes: her mother's. Sam had drawn them when they'd spent the afternoon at a little café, talking about the show, the possibilities it would open up, and what it meant for Sam's career. And she hadn't even once thought to ask why her mother looked so thin.

Sam slammed the book closed as a bitter taste filled her mouth. The fire was growing low in the grate. If she wanted to stay awake any longer, she would have to add more wood.

No. I'd better to go to bed. I'm probably just worn out from the drive and the stress. I'll start working tomorrow, when I have a clear head.

Sam threw a final regretful look at the empty canvas then returned the sketchbook to the table before climbing the stairs to the bedroom. Heat from the fire had risen to take the worst of the chill out of the upstairs room, but Sam still brushed her teeth feverishly quickly before wriggling under the multiple quilts, fully clothed.

She could see the stars through a gap in the curtains. They were so much brighter than in the city and clustered so thickly that it was almost impossible for her to think she was looking at the same sky as the one she could see from her apartment window. As she closed her eyes and felt the sluggishness of sleep grow over her, her mind returned to the man she'd seen on the dock and the way his shoulders had quivered as he gazed into the water.

CHAPTER 3

THUNK.

Sam jolted awake. Her mind was still half-full of scattered dreams, and she couldn't immediately remember where she was. Pale light streamed through the balcony's glass door, painting color across the wooden floor, and Sam struggled to get out from under Peter's layered quilts.

What was that noise? It wasn't part of my dream.

The icy early morning air assaulted her feet as soon as she swung them over the edge of the bed. Sam gasped and pulled on her sneakers with quick tugs. She wished she had a jacket, but all of her clothes were still on the ground floor.

Then the events from the previous day flooded back to her, dispelling the sleepy haze, and Sam lurched to her feet. Her skin prickled as she turned toward the stairwell.

The noise had come from the ground floor. Sam edged toward

the stairs and tried to remember if she'd locked the cabin's door. She didn't think so. Her mind immediately went to the man on the dock. *There's no way that guy hung around overnight.*

And yet, *something* had broken through her sleep. It hadn't been a quiet noise, either; it wasn't something that could be explained by the house's wood flexing in the cool or the early morning chatter of birds. Sam wished she'd had the forethought to bring the ax upstairs.

She crept down the steps, keeping her breathing and footfalls quiet. When she reached the bend at the corner of the house, she ducked her head to get a look into the lower room. It was empty.

Thank goodness.

That was one good thing about the open-plan building: it left nowhere to hide. Light came through the four windows, scattering shadows under the table and in the corners of the kitchenette. Still, Sam remained alert as she descended the stairs and stood, shivering, in the center of the room.

If I'm alone, what caused the noise?

The answer came when she glanced toward the cold fireplace. A log had fallen off the woodpile and lay on the fur rug.

Sam let her breath out in a whoosh and hurried to her travel case. She unzipped it and dug through the clothes to find her thickest jacket and a pair of hiking boots, which she swapped for her thin sneakers. It wasn't enough to stop her from shivering, so she turned toward the fireplace with the intention of lighting it.

She made it halfway across the room before she stopped. She'd been so intent on looking for a stranger in her cabin that two very important changes had escaped her notice. Firstly, there were three mugs laid out on the kitchen bench, just in front of the window overlooking the shrubs behind the cabin. She hadn't used any mugs the day before. The cups had been arranged with precision too; their handles all pointed in the same direction— toward the easel.

There, she found the second change, and it froze her breath in her lungs. Someone had painted on the canvas.

A man's face stared at her from the cloth. It was a closely cropped portrait, realistic and barely dry. Deep-set gray eyes gazed out from above a crooked nose and thin lips. He had thick salt-and-pepper hair and uneven stubble. A red mark—a cut that had not quite healed—marred his cheek.

"Oh," Sam whispered, unable to think of anything else to say. "*Oh.*"

She recognized the style. The thin strokes, the mingling of the colors, and the particular way the hair had been painted were all very familiar because she'd seen them hundreds of times before.

Either I painted this picture, or someone spent an awful lot of time and effort imitating me.

Sam struggled to slow her frantic breathing as her mind snatched at shreds of logic among the rising panic. *Am I sure I'm alone?*

The ax was leaning against the wall beside the fireplace, where she'd left it. Sam picked it up and raised it in front of her body, even though it was a struggle to keep it steady. She could think of only a couple of places an average-size person could hide, and

16

she moved through them quickly. First, she tried the kitchen pantry, which was still stacked with canned soups, pastas, and far too many cans of Spam. Next, she tried the cupboard below the stairs, where she found nothing except a stack of spare blankets and empty buckets.

Sam ran back up the stairs, staggering under the weight of the ax, and into the bedroom. She doubted anyone could have gotten up there without her noticing, but she still checked under the bed and in the wardrobe. Finally, she moved to the balcony and pulled back the thick curtains, exposing a breathtaking view of the outside world.

Mist had rolled in overnight. It covered the ground like a blanket and drifted across the lake in lazy swirls. Sam followed the low-lying clouds to where they rose against the bases of the mountain, clinging to the greenery like a ghostly spiderweb. It was one of the most eerily beautiful things she'd ever seen.

Sam exhaled, and the plume of her breath rose past her to dissolve in the icy air. It had to be early morning; there was enough light to see her way, but the sun hadn't yet topped the mountains in the distance.

Dark motion in the mist caught Sam's attention, and she turned back to the lake. When she squinted through the thick fog, she caught glimpses of... *What? The dock? No...something* on *the dock.*

Sam gasped as another billow of mist engulfed the dark shape. She didn't waste time waiting for the fog to clear, but turned, crossed the room, and took the stairs two at a time. She skidded on the main room's polished wooden floor and hit the door with a thud. Her fingers shook as she fumbled to turn the handle, then she burst through the opening, ax held high, and took two stumbling steps toward the dock.

The mist rolled around her, seeming to pull her into its folds. It was much thicker than it had looked from the upstairs room. It prickled at her cheeks and nose, freezing her lungs when she inhaled. Stepping outside was like entering another dimension; even the sounds from the forest seemed muffled. Sam squinted, searching for shapes among the sea of white as she staggered forward.

The beginning of the dock appeared first, the tar-black pillars materializing through the mist like phantom ships. Sam continued until she was even with them then put one hand on the closest pillar. The condensation that had gathered on it trickled down her wrist.

"Hello?" Sam called, but the fog seemed to swallow her voice. She shuddered and glanced at her feet, where the dark planks grew out of the grassy shore. *Peter said not to go on the dock...*

The mist thinned as a gust of wind tore through it, and Sam glimpsed the end of the dock. *Empty.* The black pillars marking the walkway's end were barely visible; beyond them, everything was white. *Is that what I saw? I suppose, in the fog and from a distance, it would be possible to mistake a post for a kneeling person.*

Even so, Sam didn't turn away immediately, but watched as the mist enveloped the dock once again. She felt, deep in her bones, that she wasn't alone. It was one of the most uncanny sensations she'd ever experienced. She let the ax drop and rested its head on the ground, keeping her fingers on the handle to stop it from tipping. Somewhere in the distance, a bird screeched, and a flurry of wings followed as it and its companions took flight. Sam turned, but the mist was too thick to see them.

It was too thick to see *anything*.

Sam tightened her shaking fingers on the ax. She kept turning, searching for a landmark, any shape at all, but all she could see was a wall of white. No trees. No cabin. *It's like I've been transported to another planet.*

The thought frightened her, and she started forward, guessing the direction of the cabin as well as she could. The ax's head dragged over the frosty, sparse grass, and for a moment, the grating noise was all she could hear. Then more birdcalls and whirring wings filled the air, and a tall, familiar outline emerged from the fog.

Thank goodness.

Sam increased her pace to a sprint and pushed through the cabin's door. It was dark inside—darker than she remembered it—but it felt *safe*, and with a sigh, she dropped the ax beside the fireplace.

There wasn't much kindling left, but she managed to light it and spent twenty minutes carefully feeding in the smallest pieces of wood until the fire was strong enough to survive without her. The sun had topped the ridge by the time she looked out the window, and she was surprised to see the fog had almost entirely disappeared. Pockets of it lingered in the corners of the mountainside, and thin wisps were rapidly dissolving from above the smooth surface of the lake.

The dock was easy to see. Its dark wood contrasted with the crisp blue, and the view looked good enough to make a decent painting.

On the subject of paintings…

Sam reluctantly turned to face the portrait in the corner of the room and met the cool-gray eyes of the strangely familiar face.

CHAPTER 4

SAM STEPPED TOWARD THE painting. The eyes transfixed her. The cruel gaze held secrets she never wanted to hear.

She couldn't remember where she knew him from. He definitely wasn't someone she was on a first-name basis with. It was a brief familiarity—like someone she'd passed in the street, whose face had been unique enough for her to subconsciously make a note of.

Her apartment was on the outskirts of the state's largest city. Sam guessed she would have passed at least a hundred new faces each day—and yet, she knew if she'd seen that face before, she wouldn't have forgotten it so easily. *Where'd it come from, then? A dream?*

Yes, she realized. *I did dream him. But not in that way.*

Images rose in her mind when she closed her eyes. She saw herself walking down the stairs and passing the fire, which had been reduced to coals. She'd taken her place in front of the easel, palette in one hand and brush in the other, and painted as though she were in a trance.

Sam pressed her palms to her forehead and rocked on her feet. *I've been sleepwalking, then. Or, rather, sleep-painting…*

She thought she remembered putting the paint in the desk drawer before returning upstairs. Sure enough, when she opened the drawer, a plastic palette sat inside, covered with well-blended colors.

It's the stress. I'm panicking about the Heritage show and the stranger in the mist, and my brain's blending the ideas and processing them the best way it can.

Sam glanced at the painting again. If it was a message from her subconscious, it didn't bode well: the haggard face; the cruel, hungry expression; and the way the deep gray eyes seemed to follow her… Sam closed the distance between herself and the painting, pulled it off the easel, and propped it against the wall so it faced the wooden planks.

The room was warming up, thanks to the fire, and Sam took off her thick coat and draped it over the back of the chair. She was ravenous. The pantry held a stack of baked bean cans hidden behind the Spam, and she tipped one of them into a blackened pan to heat over the fire.

Sam ate straight out of the pot while she warmed her dew-dampened shoes in front of the fire. By the time she'd finished eating and had washed up, the forest was alive with noises. She checked her phone; it was just after ten in the morning. *Good. Still early enough to have a productive day.*

There weren't any service bars on her mobile, but that was to be expected. She'd been watching the signal on the drive up, and it had disappeared not long before she'd entered the woods. For the rest of the trip, her phone would be a very expensive, cumbersome clock.

Sam stretched, working the tension out of her back and shoulders, then pulled the wooden dining chair up to the easel. She picked out a small canvas, one only a little larger than her head, and set it in place. A smaller canvas meant less space to fill…and less pressure to make it perfect.

She pulled the palette out of the drawer and stared at the myriad blended oil colors. She still found it hard to believe that she'd painted such a coherent image while asleep. Sam pushed the thought from her mind and dabbed her brush into the paint. It was tacky from being left in the drawer overnight, but not completely set, so she grabbed the bottle of primer and added a dollop to loosen the paint. It was an expensive brand of oils, and she didn't want to waste any more than she already had.

A large smudge of green-gray covered one corner of the palette, so Sam swirled her brush through it and raised her hand to apply it to the canvas. *Okay, Sammy, what are we painting today?*

She hesitated, the brush held a millimeter from the cloth. She hadn't planned anything, and the usual ideas seemed reluctant to enter her mind. All she could think about were the sallow face and cold gray eyes.

Focus! Pick something and put it on the canvas. It's that simple. What about a bird? You used to love painting birds.

Sam lowered the brush and looked at the rest of the colors on the palette. Dusky pink—that had been for the man's face. The gray-blue had been his flannel top. The dull green, which was currently on her brush, had been used for the trees behind him. And the deep gray, just a tiny amount, was for his irises.

Why can't I get him out of my mind?

"C'mon, Sam," she coached herself, rolling her head to relax the muscles in her neck. "Push through the block. Start freestyle. Paint abstract, even. Just get some colors on the canvas, and it'll get easier—you'll see."

Twenty minutes later, Sam carried the canvas, half-covered in haphazard smears of greens and blues, to the fireplace. She threw it onto the flames and wiped the tear tracks off her cheeks as she watched the wet paint send up plumes of black smoke. The aborted painting took far longer to burn than she was comfortable with.

"Damn it," she hissed, pressing her palms against her eyes to hold back the dampness. "Get it together, Sam. You've only got a week."

She personally knew at least three artists who would have committed first-degree murder for the chance to show their work at the Heritage Gallery. It was the sort of thing an artist put on a résumé to raise eyebrows, and the gallery had launched more careers than she could count.

Denzel, her childhood friend, was interning at the Heritage. He'd called in every favor he was owed and blended them with a lot of groveling and carefully placed hints to work the impossible: a show for Sam, a nearly unheard-of artist.

The gallery's coordinator had given Sam eight months to prepare a collection of a dozen exhibits. Eight months had seemed like an eternity at the time, but there she was, with nine days until the opening night, and nothing was ready. Nothing started. Nothing even *conceived.*

During the first week following her invite, Sam had felt as though she might explode from all of the possibilities filling her mind. She'd shared them with her mother that crisp autumn morning as they'd enjoyed their coffees at the local café. While they talked, Sam had idly sketched her companion's eyes without fully realizing how much they'd sunken in a few short weeks, how gaunt her mother's cheeks were, or how her skin seemed almost papery in the fluorescent light.

Sometimes, Sam wondered if her mother had ever intended to tell her. If she'd known, Sam could have taken time away from her job, moved back in with her mother, and spent as much of those last few days with her only remaining parent as possible. Instead, she'd had to hear it from her mother's doctor at the stroke of midnight. *"The cancer's progressed far more rapidly than we antici-pated. If you would like to say goodbye, you'll need to come quickly."*

After that, she'd had only five hours with her mother—to sit beside the hospital bed, stroking the fragile, bone-thin hand resting on starchy white sheets—before the best person in her life had exhaled for the last time.

The following weeks passed like a dream. Sam had struggled to keep the days straight, often missing her shifts at work or turning up on the wrong days. She'd stopped painting—and stopped *thinking* about painting—and the Heritage Gallery invite had been lost at the bottom of a drawer.

She'd emerged from the fog of raw grief as a different person. She still loved painting. That was built into her identity. Nothing on heaven or earth could abolish the joy a loaded brush gave her. But the desire was gone. She was like a starving man whose hunger had been sated; he could gaze at a lavish feast, appreciate its appeal, then shrug and turn away.

Then one day, she'd realized the exhibition was less than two months away, and she hadn't touched a paintbrush in half a year. Panic set in. She'd bought new canvases, new paints, and a clean set of brushes then tried to create again. The results had disgusted her. *You're just rusty,* she'd told herself as she glared at a horribly proportioned, terribly boring tree she'd created. *Practice will bring it all back.*

Except, it hadn't. She'd tried to start the show's collection a dozen times during those two months and had trashed it every time.

Two weeks out from the exhibition, when Sam had been on the verge of calling Denzel to tearfully, humiliatingly cancel, Uncle Peter had called up like her guardian angel and offered her a week at his cabin. It provided the perfect setting to get her back into her art: there was no contact with the outside world. No distractions. Nothing to do except paint.

But all I have so far is a sleep-created, nightmare-induced face. I can't even imagine what the critics would say if I tried to show that at the Heritage.

Sam watched the fire until it had reduced the canvas to a sad slop on top of the smoldering logs, then she inhaled and leaned back against the armchair. *The week's still young. Twelve paintings is a stretch, but not impossible.*

The cabin smelled awful thanks to the burning chemicals, and the stench churned her stomach. Sam glanced at the window and caught a glimpse of rich green trees and blue skies. The day was too beautiful to spend indoors. *Maybe a taste of nature will give me the kick I need.*

The idea energized her, and Sam pulled on a thin jacket and packed her sketchbook and a box of charcoal pencils into her satchel. She added a water bottle then left the cabin, locking the door on the way out.

The lake's shore looked worlds away from the ethereal visage she'd walked through that morning. Straggly brown-green grass grew in patches among the sand that led into the still water. Sam turned right and followed the curving shore around the lake.

About a kilometer along, the steep mountain to her right softened into a slope. Sam made out an overgrown trail leading into the trees and picked up her pace as she entered it. The trees and vines grew high over her, blocking out almost all of the sunlight, but not even the shade could spare her as the day warmed and the uphill climb made her uncomfortably hot. She stripped off her jacket and tied it around her waist.

The brush became increasingly thick and snaggly as she moved higher. Vines caught at her clothes and twisted across the dirt path, threatening to trip her. She had to stop several times to remove thorns from her hair.

Then the path turned, and Sam found herself facing an open, rocky area. It looked as though a landslide had occurred there a few years back, and it had cleared a gap in the vegetation. Sam climbed one of the higher rocks and settled down to rest on its flat top.

The forest spread out like a green carpet ahead of her, rushing to meet the blue water. She'd traveled farther than she'd expected, and Sam couldn't stop a grin from growing over her face as she spotted her cabin, laughably small, at the edge of the lake.

She closed her eyes and drank in the sensations. The cold rock beneath her was refreshing. Dead and dried leaves under her feet crackled whenever she shifted. Birds screamed in the distance, and insects hummed in the foliage.

Sam pulled the art book out of her satchel. The Heritage's show would need proper canvas paintings, but at least she could sketch some ideas to use as references. She swiveled her wrist to loosen it, then started to draw anything in sight: trees, rocks, leaves, and even her own boots.

A brightly colored bird flitted out of the bushes and hopped across the rocks. Sam kept her hand moving but held her breath as she watched the bird. It either hadn't seen her or didn't mind the company as it foraged for insects among the fallen leaves. Then something startled it—Sam couldn't tell if she was guilty or not—and the bird dashed away with a shrill cry.

Sam sighed and glanced at her art book. Shock hit her like a cold slap. In the center of the paper, surrounded by scribbled plants and indistinct shapes, was a drawing of the man.

CHAPTER 5

SAM COULDN'T BELIEVE WHAT she was seeing. The pencil fell from her grip and hit the forest floor with a dull *tk*, but she barely noticed. The face was looser and messier, but clearly recognizable.

I can't believe I drew that.

Sam closed the art book with a snap, simultaneously creeped out and ashamed. She didn't want to dwell on the image, where she knew the face from, or why her subconscious was bringing it up all of a sudden. The calm, happy mood she'd developed during the hike had dissipated as thoroughly as if someone had thrown water over her.

She packed up her equipment and turned back to the trail. Going left would lead her downhill, toward the cabin, but the path also continued to her right, weaving into the thickening forest. Sam hesitated then turned right. *Now that I'm here, I may as well see where it leads.*

The path took her up the steep incline, zigzagging through the trees so erratically that Sam started to regret her decision to follow it. Just when she was about to give it up as a futile exercise, the path opened onto a proper hiking trail.

Sam stopped in the middle of the cleared area and took a deep breath, glad to be out of the claustrophobically tight vegetation. She couldn't see any nearby signs, so she turned right and followed the new trail across the length of the mountain.

Occasionally, the path opened onto a lookout with a view of the lake. The cabin was no longer visible, but Sam caught glimpses of hillsides that the curve of the mountains had previously hidden. She followed the trail for a little more than twenty minutes before encountering a blockade. A chain crossed the path, tethered at each end to a metal pole. A placard—facing away from her—hung from its center.

Sam climbed over the chain to read the sign and frowned.

TRAIL CLOSED—UNSAFE

The path she'd followed had been wide and well maintained. *What's unsafe about it?*

A little way ahead of her, the dirt road melted into a clearing. Several other trails split off from it, and a large sign displaying a map stood in the clearing's center. Sam approached the map and let her eyes rove over the maze of trails circling the lake and surrounding mountains before she spotted a little red marker reading *You Are Here.*

She traced the paths leading out from her location and found only one that went near Uncle Peter's cabin: the closed one.

Well, at least that means I'll have some privacy.

She thought of the man kneeling on the dock, and shivers crawled down her spine. It was too late to visit any of the other trails, so she turned back to the chained-off path. She had one leg over the barricade when a voice made her jump.

"Ma'am, I'm going to have to ask you to stop."

Sam nearly tripped over the chain but managed to right herself in time to see the uniformed ranger jogging out of one of the side paths. "That's a restricted area."

Color rose across Sam's face. "Sorry—I know—I'm, uh…"

He came to a stop in front of her, breathing deeply but not quite panting. His ranger's uniform, dark green with gold highlights, was well pressed and clean. Sam felt as though she were being scrutinized, but it was hard to tell thanks to the dark sunglasses he wore under his cap.

"Where're you coming from, ma'am?" His voice was clipped, but not accusatory, and Sam managed to form a coherent answer through her embarrassment and shock.

"Sorry—I came from that path. I didn't know it was restricted. I'm staying in the cabin by the lake."

The ranger cocked his head to one side. "Not Peter Mahoney's place?"

"That's it, yeah. I'm his niece."

"Well then." A grin grew across the ranger's sharp jaw, and he took off his glasses. He had bright-blue eyes, which sparkled with

31

faint amusement. "I suppose an apology is in order. I know Pete. He's a good guy. He helped out during the burn-offs last year. I didn't know the cabin was occupied, that's all."

"I'm only staying a week." Sam glanced at the trail behind her. "Is it okay for me to go back that way?"

"Sure thing. Just be careful. There've been some accidents along that path lately. Don't stray into the forest, and watch out for falling rocks, okay?"

Sam nodded. She couldn't imagine how the flat, orderly trail could be any more dangerous than the others crisscrossing the mountains, but then, maybe the problem section came farther along, past where she turned off onto the smaller path leading to the cabin.

An idea struck her, and she glanced back at the ranger. "Uh, if you don't mind me asking…"

"Go right ahead, ma'am." He'd relaxed and was watching her with evident amusement.

Sam wondered if she looked as sweaty and disheveled as she felt. She tried to stand a little taller, hoping he wouldn't notice her embarrassed flush. "Are there any properties on the lake? Other than Peter's, I mean."

His eyebrows rose. "Now that's an odd question. Not as far as I know. From what I heard, Peter was friendly with a couple of the councilmen, which is how he got permission to build there. Otherwise, the whole area is government owned. But then, I'm only in charge of the northern region of the forest. The lake itself is a state issue."

"Right." Sam turned toward the path, but the ranger stopped her. "Why the question, ma'am?"

She hesitated, wondering how much to tell him. "It's just…a man was hanging around the dock in front of the property last night. I wasn't sure if he lived in the area or was a hiker, but, uh…" She trailed off and waved a hand toward the chain's sign.

The ranger's face was unreadable, but the businesslike clip had returned to his voice. "Well, I can't discount that someone climbed over the chain. I try to keep an eye on it, but there's only so much time I can spend around this area."

"Right. Of course."

"You haven't seen anyone since then, have you?"

Sam thought of the dark shape barely visible through the swirling fog that morning. "No."

"Hmm." The ranger watched her for a moment, a slight frown hovering over his blue eyes, then he unclipped a black box from his belt. "Better safe than sorry. Take my walkie-talkie; it's the only thing that can be used to communicate around here unless you have a two-way radio. This'll get you direct communication with the ranger's station, though, and there's almost always someone there if you need help."

"Oh!" Sam took the black box and smiled at it. "Hey, thanks."

"No problem. Drop it off at the office when you leave, okay? My boss would kill me if I lost it."

"Sure, I'll do that."

The ranger flashed her another smile as he tipped his hat. "You have a nice day, ma'am."

He watched her as she climbed over the fence and didn't turn away until the curve of the path hid her from sight.

CHAPTER 6

THE WALK UP TO the clearing had taken three hours. The hike back down seemed to take twice as long. By the time she stepped onto the lakeshore, Sam was exhausted and famished. She felt incredibly stupid for walking so far with only a bottle of water.

The sun was already passing behind the high mountains when she stumbled into the cabin and tugged off her boots. She massaged the blister that had formed on her right foot, then, grumbling to herself, she snatched up the more comfortable sneakers.

The cabin had retained a lot of the heat from the now-dead fire, but she knew the warmth wouldn't last long as night set in. She toyed with the idea of going straight to bed without bothering to rekindle the fire, but she knew she would regret it when she had to get up in the freezing morning. *Besides, I could really go for some hot soup right now.*

That meant she would need kindling. Sam sighed and tied the sneakers, tossed her satchel onto the table, and left the comfort of the cabin. She turned toward the forest, aiming for the closest crop of trees, but a flash of motion in her peripheral vision stopped her. She turned so quickly that she nearly slipped in the gritty sand, but there was nothing to see: just the empty dock and the glassy water.

Sam approached the pier, keeping her senses on high alert. She could have sworn she'd seen something move on it. *The man came back*, her mind insisted. But the dock was empty, and there was nowhere for a person to hide—without jumping into the lake, which was impossible. The water was still.

The sensation of no longer being alone, the same one she'd felt when she'd arrived, washed over her. Sam hesitated at the base of the dock, scanning the shore, the still water, the gently swaying trees, and the clear patch surrounding the cabin.

You're alone, she told herself, trying to convince her frantic, galloping heart. *There's no one for miles.*

An exhale, so faint that she could barely hear it over the drum of her pulse, seemed to rush through her. It sounded raw and raspy, as though the air had been pulled through a damaged throat.

You imagined it. There's nothing. Nothing except the wind in the trees and your stupid imagination going wild—

She could feel eyes on her, watching her, quietly delighted to see while not being seen.

Stop it, stop it, stop it—

35

Then an owl, tired of waiting for the sun to finish its descent behind the mountains, screeched. Sam jumped. She was shocked to find she'd been holding her breath, and she drew in a lungful of oxygen with a deep shudder. The lake was still. The shore was empty. It was getting dark, and she had a fire to start.

Shaky and a little embarrassed, Sam hurried toward the forest. An abundance of small, dry sticks lay among the fallen leaves, and Sam gathered an armful before returning to the cabin. There was still plenty of wood in the bracket beside the fireplace, so Sam locked the cabin's door and settled down for the night as the last of the sunlight disappeared over the ridge.

The soup—two cans of chicken and vegetables heated over the fire—was delicious. Sam sipped at it as she rubbed her aching feet over the plush fireside rug. She wished she'd brought a novel. While packing for the trip, she'd imagined herself consumed with creative inspiration and painting late into the night, but she was starting to realize how unrealistic that was. After her day of hiking, she couldn't tolerate even the idea of trying to work. All she wanted was to lounge in front of the fire and watch a movie or lose herself in a good book.

She'd searched the cupboards in the vague hope that Peter would have brought a book on one of his weekend trips, but all she'd come up with was a technical manual for lacquering techniques, a pack of cards, and the radio he'd mentioned in his letter.

The radio was better than nothing, so Sam filled it with batteries and turned it on. It caught only one station, but she supposed she shouldn't have been surprised. She was so far out from civilization that she was lucky to have even that. It seemed to be a variety station that ran interviews, programs it had obviously bought from larger stations, songs she'd never heard before, and even the serialized reading of a novel.

Sam put the empty pot on the floor beside her chair and relaxed into the cushions. She closed her eyes as she listened to the presenter—a man with an old, crackly voice, who called himself Uncle Earnest—read that evening's news.

It was the standard fare: politicians bickering over a new bill, a natural disaster threatening a country on the other side of the globe, and an update on the Green Energy project. Sam let the words drift over her, feeling strangely detached from the events affecting the rest of the world.

"And now for some local news," Uncle Earnest said. There was a pause as he rustled through his papers.

Sam felt her eyes start to drift closed as she watched the fire spit up sparks.

"For those fine souls in Spring Valley, you'll be happy to know the dam has been successfully repaired, and your homes are once again safe. We've had another report of a giant panther sighting, this time in Clearview. And for any of you good folk living near Harob Lake—"

Sam's eyes snapped open.

"Police have called off the search for Ian McCarthy nearly two weeks after his disappearance. He's the fifth this year, so take care if you plan to visit the lake. Up next, we have some local talent, Jamie and the Spitfires, performing a song of their own creation, 'Dreaming of Hills.' Enjoy!"

The country ballad was completely uninspired and sung by a nasally teenager, but Sam barely noticed. She sat completely still, hands clenched on the chair's armrests, staring at the radio. *Fifth this year... Does he mean it's the fifth disappearance? Was Ian a tourist, or did he live near here? And what part of Harob Lake?* Remembering the chain across the trail, Sam shivered. She felt in her pockets for her mobile to call Uncle Peter, then remembered it didn't have any reception.

The cabin felt simultaneously too small and too large. The fire brightened and warmed the area immediately in front of it, but leaping shadows dominated the rest of the room. Sam went to the kitchen, felt in the drawer for the candles she'd seen there the previous day, and lit five of them, placing them on plates in strategic locations around the room. They helped a little, but not enough to keep her from shivering as she returned to the fire.

The dreadful country song finished, and Uncle Earnest introduced a segment on financial planning. Sam threw a fresh log on the fire then coiled in the chair, wrapping her arms around her torso. The next news segment would be in an hour; if she was lucky, Earnest would share more details about Ian McCarthy. In the meantime, she could let the trite talk programs and country music distract her.

CHAPTER 7

THE RADIO WAS STILL playing when Sam woke the next morning. She'd collapsed sideways in the chair, and her neck and back ached from the awkward position. She pulled herself upright with a groan and tried to stretch some of the soreness out.

Light streamed through the cracks in the curtains, splashing long strips of gold across the wooden floor. The fire had reduced to embers, leaving the air brisk, but not as cold as it otherwise would have been.

The radio was playing a morning program that felt a little too chirpy and energetic to match Sam's emotions, so she fumbled with the contraption until she managed to turn it off. Silence rushed in to take its place. Sam sighed and drew a hand through her hair. She felt greasy and gritty, and desperately needed a shower. She'd meant to have one the previous night, before bed, but nothing about that day had gone according to plan.

Then she glanced about the room and did a double take. A new painting sat on the easel. Sam's stagnant heart rate spiked, and shaking off her grogginess, she crossed the room in three paces.

Once again, her own hand had clearly made the brush strokes. The painting depicted a moonlit forest scene. Sick, strangely shaped trees clustered on either side of an overgrown path. Striding down the path, his grim gray eyes staring out from the paint and an ax clasped in his right hand, was the man.

Sam closed her eyes and rubbed her palms across her temples. The memories were hazy and dreamlike, but she recalled approaching the easel, squeezing paint onto the palette, blending, dabbing, and drawing stripes of color across the canvas. She'd then left the cups on the bench before returning to the fireside chair.

She turned toward the kitchen. Sure enough, two cups stood in front of the sink, their handles pointing at the easel. *There were three yesterday. Is that significant, or is it just my dream-self getting lazy?*

Sam plucked the painting off the easel, intending to lean it against the wall next to its companion, and froze. A second, smaller painting rested behind the first. The image was set underwater, facing the surface. The dark water was swirling and full of bubbles. It was less detailed than the previous images—more rushed, almost as if she'd been frantic when creating it—but the moon, shining through the frenzy, was unmistakable.

"Jeez," Sam hissed. Like with the first painting, she turned both of the new ones so they faced the wall.

What on earth possessed me to create stuff like this? Is it really from stress? Because I've had plenty of stress over the last year, and all it's done is wear down my immune system. Maybe that's the point, though. Maybe this holiday is letting me reacquaint myself with my feelings, and it's like opening a floodgate. These could be repressed emotions spilling onto the canvas. Damn. Wish they'd spill in a more cohesive, marketable way.

Sam found the palette in the drawer and rinsed the half-dried paint down the sink. The water, fresh from the tank behind the cabin, was ice cold. *I'd probably die if I tried to bathe in this.* Sam turned toward the fireplace and scrunched her nose when she saw only two small pieces of wood left in the bracket. *Not enough to heat water* and *cook breakfast.*

Sam pulled on her boots and heavy jacket and pushed open the door. It was later than she'd thought; the sun was already above the mountains. The mist had all but disappeared, though it had left the grass damp. The lake was stunning; its smooth water reflected the fluffy white clouds trailing across the sky and the rich-green mountains. The dock was empty, but the water just beyond it rippled, probably from a fish that had become a little too enthusiastic in the morning light.

Sam jogged the dozen paces between the cabin and the small shed and wrenched open its door. The inside was exactly how she'd imagined it: a haven for a mountain man at heart. A workbench ran along one wall, covered with sanders, grinders, circular saws, and goodness knew what else. A canoe rested on a pallet, taking up most of the right side of the shed. Sam ran her hand across the dark wood appreciatively. *I'd love to take this out on the lake before the week's over.*

The huge stack of firewood waited for her at the back of the shed. A wheelbarrow lay next to it, and Sam hurried to load it up with the logs then pulled it out of the shed. When she turned toward the cabin, the ripples hadn't disappeared from the lake. In fact, they'd intensified.

Water frothed and churned as something struggled just under the surface. The ripples, which had at first lapped peacefully against the shore, were battering at it, surging forward and retreating like small waves.

Sam stared, her mouth open. She couldn't see what was causing the disturbance, but it had to be big. *What kinds of fish live in this lake?*

The water roiled, spraying droplets high into the air. Dark mud, drawn up from the lake's floor, stained the crystal-blue water black, slowly bleeding out from the frenzy.

Then, as though a switch had been flicked, it stopped. The miniature waves bumped into the dock's pillars and spent themselves on the shore as the lake's surface stilled.

Sam dropped the wheelbarrow and approached the water's edge. The disturbance had been just past the dock. If she stood on the end of the pier, she might be able to see the cause.

Don't go onto the dock. The phrase from Peter's letter echoed in her head as she eyed the wood. It looked solid. But her uncle *had* underlined his warning twice.

Caution won out, and Sam reluctantly returned to her burden.

The wood had spilled when she'd dropped the wheelbarrow, and she grumbled as she righted and refilled it.

It only took a few minutes to transfer the logs into the bracket beside the fireplace, then Sam returned the wheelbarrow to the shed. She kept one eye on the water as she passed the lake, but it didn't repeat its antics.

Bathing in the wilderness was a new experience for Sam. She heated pots of water over the fire, carried them upstairs to the bathtub, and mixed in enough cold water from the pump to bring it to a tolerable temperature. She'd forgotten to bring soap, so she used shampoo instead. It wasn't until she'd drained the dirty water that she realized she'd forgotten to boil anything to rinse herself with. She swore under her breath, pumped a few bursts of the icy tank water into the tub, and splashed it over herself as quickly as she could.

She was shivering by the time she drained the bath for the second time and wrapped herself in the two towels she'd brought. Sam hurried downstairs to where the fire crackled pleasantly and warmed herself while she dried her hair.

It was past lunch by the time she'd finished dressing, and she set to exploring the depths of the pantry. She decided it wasn't a day to be healthy, so she pushed the beans, Spam, and canned vegetables to one side and eventually settled on a cup of instant noodles.

Sam planned her day while she ate. She had less than four hours of daylight left. Part of her wanted to pull the canoe out from the shed and take a spin on the lake, but she squashed the idea quickly. Whatever had stirred up the water must have been strong, and there was no guarantee that being in a canoe would keep her safe. Insane ideas rose in the back of her mind—*What if the lake has freshwater sharks or even Harob's own version of the Loch Ness Monster?*—and even though she could laugh at them, she couldn't entirely dismiss them.

The second reason against going onto the lake was the entire purpose of the trip: she had five days left to create twelve paintings. Time wasn't in her favor.

Sam washed up quickly then set a fresh canvas onto the easel. She laid her best set of oils on the table, opened her favorite roll of brushes, and stared at the blank cloth.

Okay, Sam, what are we painting? The gray eyes flashed into her mind, but she pushed them back out. *Nope, not today. How about a corrupted classic? They're a little cheesy, but at least they won't be met with complete derision by the art elite.*

Sam took a soft pencil and sketched the faint outline of a bowl of fruit onto the canvas. She didn't have any references, but she thought it came out reasonably well. She added some maggots crawling out of the apple and dripping onto the crocheted cloth below the bowl, then squeezed the appropriate oil colors onto her palette.

The painting started well. She applied the dark colors first then built up to the light. The bowl was steel gray. *The same gray as his eyes*, she realized, before continuing hurriedly. She used slightly off colors for the fruit. Twenty minutes later, she stepped back from the painting and felt distaste scrunch her lips. The perspective was weird, and she wasn't sure how to fix it. Sam gritted her teeth and switched to painting the background, which was normally the easiest part for her. The lines kept coming out crooked, though, no matter how often she painted over them.

"Damn it," she hissed, dropping the brush back onto the palette. "Get a grip."

It's the water. I can't get it out of my head. The way it churned and dug up mud…I've got to know what's in there.

"Fine," she said, letting her frustration bleed into decisive action. "Fine. We'll take a look at the creepy lake then. We'll prove there's nothing to be frightened of, and when we come back, we'll be able to focus on our work. Okay? Okay."

45

CHAPTER 8

THE LAKE WAS PERFECTLY still when Sam left the cabin. She went to the shed, unlocked it, and began dragging the canoe off its pallet.

It was much heavier than she'd anticipated. She got the boat off its stand without too much effort, but pulling it to the water's edge exhausted her. Sam left it on the shore while she returned to the cabin, changed into her swimsuit, and collected one of the still-damp towels. She retrieved the paddle from the shed, tossed it and the towel inside the canoe, then gave it one final, hard shove into the lake. As soon as it came free from the shore, it started drifting away, and Sam hurried after it, wading waist deep before catching its edge. The water was cold, and the sandy lake floor felt slimy between her toes. Sam grimaced, imagining the multitude of tiny creatures that were probably flittering around her feet.

She nearly tipped the canoe the first time she tried to pull herself into it, but eventually, she managed to haul herself over its edge and collapsed inside. The vessel rocked wildly, and Sam waited until it had stilled before climbing into the seat, wrapping the towel around her waist, and picking up the paddle.

She had never been canoeing before, but it had looked easy enough in the commercials she'd seen on TV. She dipped her paddle into the water and pushed a little too hard. The canoe rocked again as it turned.

"Easy," Sam muttered, switching the paddle to the opposite side and trying to ignore the sensation of cold water dripping down her arms. It took a few minutes for her to figure out a system, but then the boat started moving forward, slowly at first, but picking up speed as she alternated sides every two strokes.

Sam turned her canoe toward the end of the dock and drew as close as she dared. The worst of the sediment had cleared since that morning, but the water was still cloudy. Sam squinted, trying to make out shapes through the haze, but it was impossible.

Whatever it was probably moved on ages ago anyway.

Sam turned the boat toward the opposite side of the lake and picked up speed. She was starting to love the sway of the canoe, the splashing noises the paddle made each time she drew it through the water, and the way the breeze cut through the sun's heat. The lake was too wide to travel to the opposite end and back before the sun dipped behind the mountains, but Sam reached the halfway point before reluctantly turning around.

The cabin stood out like a dark rock against the gray-green

woods. It was the first time Sam had seen the mountains behind her home clearly, and she soaked in the view. She could see a crop of rocks halfway up the hill that she thought might have been where she'd stopped during the previous day's hike. Farther up and to the right was a slight gap in the trees—probably one of the viewing spots from the trail. Not far above her cabin, a craggy ledge jutted out from the mountain.

And on the ledge stood a man.

Sam's mouth opened in a silent gasp. The stranger's pose was stiff, except for his arms, which hung limply at his sides. He was too far away for her to see him clearly, but Sam thought he seemed tall and lean and wore dark clothes.

Calm down. It's just a hiker. So what if he ignored the warning sign and crossed over the chain? I'm sure plenty of people do that. It's not like he's the same man who was on the dock or anything. He wasn't carrying a backpack or equipment, though.

The man turned his head, and Sam followed his gaze. He was looking at the cabin. Sam's heart fluttered, but some primitive instinct told her to keep still.

Then the man looked back at the lake, and Sam felt their eyes meet. *I'll bet they're gray*, she thought as her stomach turned cold.

The man held the gaze for half a minute then turned and disappeared into the forest.

Sam sucked in a deep breath. Panic, hot and irrational, coursed through her. She began paddling as a sense of urgency overwhelmed her. *How long would it take him to reach the cabin? Could he get there first if he ran?*

Her arms ached as seldom-used muscles were taxed, but Sam pushed herself to move the canoe as fast as she was capable, single-mindedly focused on getting to the safety of the cabin and the reassuringly heavy ax.

The familiar hum of insects filled her ears as she drew closer to the shore. Sam's eyes were scanning the mountain, searching for movement between the trees, and she didn't notice immediately when her paddle snagged in a patch of weeds. The plants nearly tugged the paddle out of her hands, but she twisted in her seat and managed to keep her grip. That turned out to be a mistake. The force of the abrupt stop, combined with the way she'd turned her body, tipped the canoe and plunged her into the water.

The lake was ice-cold. Sam thrashed, trying to right herself. Her limbs brushed through the dense weeds, and their slimy leaves made her gasp as they swept over exposed skin. Water rushed into her mouth, but she bit down on it before it could fill her lungs. Her feet couldn't find the floor. A flicker of sunlight penetrated the dark water, and Sam struggled toward it, her lungs burning, her heart thundering.

Panic had clouded her mind, and she didn't see the shadowy shape drifting above her. Instead of breaking through the surface, her head rushed up to meet the canoe's hull. Sparks of light shot across her vision, and water filled her lungs as she cried out. Her limbs felt heavier than rocks; she tried to move them, but they only weighted her down, pulling her deeper into the lake. The canoe drifted in front of the sparkling sunlight, leaving her smothered in the weed-choked, muddy shadows.

Hands crept out from between the dense water plants. Ghost white and bone thin, they caressed her skin, tangled in her hair, and tugged at her ankles. There were dozens of them. Sam had a vague idea that they should have bothered her, but all she cared about was finding the energy to take another breath as the blackness crept across her vision.

CHAPTER 9

SAM WOKE IN THE cabin, lying on the rug in front of the dying fire. Her lungs felt sore, and stabbing pains extended from a spot just above her temple. She tried to sit up but thought better of it as her stomach threatened to empty itself.

How'd I get here?

Keeping her head as still as possible, Sam let her eyes rove around the room. Everything was quiet. She seemed to be alone.

A new painting stood on the easel. Someone—*I?*—had painted over the malformed fruit still life. The steel gray bowl had been turned into a large rock, and the draping background fabric had become trees, while the tabletop had been altered into bushy vegetation.

In place of the rotting fruit stood a man. It was a familiar image. She'd seen it earlier that day, albeit from a distance.

Although she hadn't been able to see the man clearly from her canoe, she'd painted him the familiar, haggard, sallow face that had been haunting her.

As soon as she thought she had control over her body, Sam staggered to her feet. She was dizzy, but all of her limbs seemed to work. She hobbled to the door and tried the handle—it had been locked from the inside. She unbolted the latch, opened the door a crack, and looked outside. The canoe rested on the shore, with one end barely touching the smooth water. She couldn't see any other signs of interference.

Sam closed and relocked the door. The ax still stood beside the fireplace, but unwilling to trust herself with it, she picked one of the paring knives out of the kitchen drawer instead. The blade was far too small to look even remotely threatening, but Sam still held it ahead of herself as she clambered up the stairs.

It only took a minute to search the bedroom and assure herself that she was definitely alone. She returned downstairs, tossed the knife toward the kitchen, and slumped into one of the overstuffed lounge chairs. Too physically drained to even cry, she watched the fireplace's glowing embers fade into ash.

She slipped into a tenuous, disjointed dream. She saw herself pulling the canoe out of the river, locking herself in the cabin, and painting as blood dripped down her face. Every time she stirred toward wakefulness, she felt the man in the painting watching her, his cold gray eyes fixed on the back of her head with an animalistic hunger.

It was dark when Sam pulled herself together enough to light the candles and draw a drink from the pump by the sink. She leaned on the bench while she savored the taste of the cold, clean water and tried to clear her head.

She didn't seem seriously hurt. Her vision wasn't blurry, and the dizziness had passed following her nap, so she doubted she was in imminent danger of brain damage. She let her mind drift to less certain ideas.

A man had been watching her from the rock. The following hours were foggy, but she was certain of that at least. She'd assumed he was a hiker stopping to admire the view, but she felt less confident of that as she remembered the way he'd glanced toward the cabin, as though he'd known exactly where to look. That, combined with the figure she'd seen on the dock and the nightmarish paintings she'd been creating in her sleep, made her deeply uneasy.

Sam approached the table. Among the jumble of paint boxes, pencils, and papers, she found the black walkie-talkie the ranger had given her.

It seemed simple enough; a red button sat on top, next to a dial to adjust the volume. *It's got to be after six. There's probably no one at the office.*

Sam pressed the button and cautiously said, "Hello?"

To her surprise, the speaker crackled when she released the button, and a terse female voice answered, "This is the Harob Park Rangers Office. Who's speaking, please?"

"Oh." Sam had been hoping to get straight through to the ranger she'd met the previous day and wasn't sure she wanted to explain her concerns to the unexpectedly cold voice. She cleared her throat and pressed the button again. "Hi, my name's Sam. I'm staying in the cabin by the lake. I spoke to a ranger yesterday, and he gave me his walkie-talkie—is he available, please?"

A *tsk* of irritation came from the speakers. "Would that have been Brandon or Tom?"

"Uh…I'm not sure, sorry. He didn't tell me his name."

"Probably Brandon," the woman said, more to herself than Sam. "He's already left for the day. Do you need emergency assistance?"

Sam felt unsteady on her feet, so she dropped onto the couch and wet her lips. The woman's voice was cold. *Unfeeling.* Still, hostile help was better than no help, so she said, "I heard on the radio that there have been disappearances around Harob Lake."

"Yes," the woman said after a brief pause. "There have been missing-person cases. They occur in any inhospitable region that's frequented by tourists."

"Were any of them found?"

Another *tsk*. "The forest spans more than eighteen square kilometers, much of it mountainous and uncharted. We make every effort to locate missing persons, but the odds are very much against us."

Sam's mouth was dry. She licked her lips again. "So…no? You didn't find them? Not even their bodies?"

"Look," the woman said, and the walkie-talkie's crackle

couldn't mask her irritation. "We maintain the trails and post signs, but there's very little we can do if an inexperienced hiker strays off the paths and becomes lost."

Sam knew her companion's patience was wearing thin, but she couldn't stop herself from saying, "The path going near my cabin was cordoned off. Is it because people have gone missing on it? More than normal, I mean?"

"I'm not at liberty to discuss the details of unresolved cases." The ranger's voice could have frozen hell. "But I can assure you, provided you take proper safety precautions when hiking, you are at no greater risk than in any other remote, densely wooded area. Now, if there's nothing else I can help you with, I would appreciate it if we could keep this line clear in case of actual emergencies."

"Oh, yeah, sure. Sorry." Sam let the walkie-talkie fall silent. She sat for a long time, staring at the empty fireplace, chewing over her options. The woman's refusal to answer was almost as good as an affirmative: the trail had been closed because people had gone missing on it, and they considered it too dangerous to keep open. Not that it had bothered the mysterious hiker.

I could leave, Sam thought as she stared at the three paintings propped against the wall, their ghastly images facing away so that she wouldn't have to see them.

Part of her wanted to go—to get out of the cloistered forest and back to her familiar, overpopulated city—but she knew she'd never forgive herself if she did. She'd been so grateful for the week in the cabin; it was a merciful lifeline, a final chance to prepare for the Heritage and save her reputation and budding career. She couldn't throw it away just because a hiker didn't like obeying caution signs.

Still, the missing-person cases bothered her.

Sam stretched to shake some of the soreness out of her shoulders and back. The candles were doing a poor job of lighting the cabin, and cold night air was starting to creep in. Sam was acutely aware of how lonely the night felt, so she turned on the radio while she lit the fire.

Uncle Earnest was back, his scratchy voice introducing his eclectic range of songs and talk shows. Sam was tipping a can of minestrone soup into a pot when he said, "Don't forget, if you have a tip or a news story you'd like to share with our listeners, you can call us on—"

Damn, wish my phone had reception. I bet he'd be more than happy to share what he knows about the missing hikers.

"Or," Earnest continued, "if you have a two-way radio, you can reach us on the following frequency..."

Sam gasped. She might not have a mobile, but the radio *was* two-way. She shoved her dinner onto the bench and ran to the black box.

CHAPTER 10

SAM MANAGED TO CONNECT just as Earnest finished introducing a bizarre disco song. She turned the radio's volume down and held her breath.

"Well, hello!" Earnest said after a moment. He sounded delighted. Sam wondered how often he had callers. "How's tonight treating you, darlin'?"

Could be better. "Fine, thanks. Uh, I've been listening to your show, and yesterday you said something about the police calling off the search—"

"For Ian McCarthy? Yes, yes, that's right. Dreadful tragedy. Are you familiar with him?"

Just as she'd hoped, Earnest was keen to talk. Sam mumbled a vague question, and the radio host happily launched into his story.

"Oh, yes, he's the fifth one this year. *Only* this year, mind.

There were another four last year, and the rangers' office won't tell me how many there were the year before. It's a dreadful thing. Often they're inexperienced hikers, see, but not always. Ian, for instance, had been hiking for decades. I watched an interview with his family. They say he was very cautious about where he went. I suppose he hadn't heard the rumors about Trail T-1."

"Trail T-1?" Sam prompted.

"That's the trail that loops down the southern side of Harob Lake. It's where almost all of the disappearances have happened. Apparently, the council cordoned it off when Ian didn't return, though it's technically no more dangerous than any other trail over the mountains. The rangers say it's a string of *bad luck*." Earnest snorted to show how little he believed in luck. "Want to know what I think?"

Sam's knuckles were white from gripping the edge of the table. "Yes, please."

"Hold on, the song's finishing. Be back in a moment, darlin'."

Sam gritted her teeth and waited for Earnest to finish introducing a new song. When he came back, his voice was muffled as though he had something in his mouth. *Is he eating his dinner?*

"Right, so we were talking about Trail T-1, weren't we? Yeah, well, these missing person cases only started about eighteen years ago. Before then, it had been decades since a soul had gone missing around that part of the lake. Then Michael Paluhik and his friends went off the trail."

There were slurping noises as Earnest drank. Sam wanted to believe it was only soda.

"Michael was one of those intense kids, y'know? From what I can gather, he was bullied as a child, but did okay for himself during his teenage years. He had trouble holding down jobs. Some people say he was fired five times in three years, others say it's three in five, and still others say he wasn't fired, but quit every time. Either way, he ended up unemployed at age twenty-six and organized a backpacking trip with two of his friends. They'd only been at it for two weeks when they decided to take a detour and hike through one of the iconic Harob Forest trails. Can you guess which one?"

"Trail T-1," Sam breathed, the image of the swinging warning sign fluttering through her mind.

"Bingo. Michael and his companions were seen entering the trail, but they never came back out."

"Wait." Sam rubbed at her eyes, which were becoming dry and irritated in the fire's light. "How come you use Michael's name, but not his companions'? What's special about him?"

"Because they never found his body," Earnest said patiently. "His two buddies, Troy and Evan, both turned up after three weeks. Badly decomposed, of course, and mostly eaten away by scavengers and insects. They were found a long way off the trail, but even though searches for Michael continued, his body remains lost. Oh, damn it—I missed the song's end. Hang on. Gotta get the botany interview set up."

Sam found it increasingly hard to be patient as her eccentric host spent two rambling minutes discussing his love for hyacinths before starting the prerecorded interview. He paused

59

to take another long, loud swig before saying, "Sorry, what were we talking about again?"

His voice was definitely starting to slur. Sam suspected the drinking was a nightly ritual for him. She wondered how long he normally managed to maintain the show before becoming completely incoherent.

"They never found Michael's body?" she prompted.

"That's right," he said, a little too enthusiastic. "And that started a spate of missing people. And missing bodies. What I mean to say is, the people went missing, and their bodies couldn't be found."

"Right," Sam said, trying, and failing, to follow his logic. "And you think it's all tied to Michael—"

"It's all *because* of Michael, darlin'! Don't you see? His soul can't rest as long as his body is missing. He's become a, uh, not a regular ghost, but one of the overcharged ghosts. What do you call them? Poltergeists. That's it. He's become a poltergeist."

"Ah." Sam squeezed her lips together as she tried to decide whether she wanted to laugh or groan. "Of course."

"I'm glad you have an open mind," Earnest said, completely missing the disappointed note in Sam's voice. "A lot of people balk as soon as they hear the word *ghost*. But it explains *everything*. Have you heard the rumors about a mysterious, shadowed figure that stalks through the woods? They're not just rumors. I bumped into one of the rangers at the pub last week. Nice guy, y'know, but he looked pretty shaken up. After a bit of prodding, he told me why. He'd been helping look for Ian McCarthy. The search parties were all called off at sundown—it's too dangerous to be stumbling through the woods in the dark, yeah?—but this ranger had stayed on a bit longer. He knew the pathways well enough and had enough hiking experience to keep reasonably safe, so he continued searching until just after night had fallen. He said he was on his way back to the base when he saw a dark figure watching him from between the trees."

Sam frowned at the radio. She wasn't sure what to make of the story; Uncle Earnest was clearly a good way to being drunk, but he also sounded sincere.

"Well," the radio host continued, completely oblivious that the brief gardening interview had ended and his station was broadcasting silence, "he said it was the shock of his life. He called out to the figure, but it turned around and—these are his own words, mind—melted into the trees. For a moment, he thought it might be Ian, so he followed, but pretty quickly realized it couldn't be the missing hiker. Ian had red hair, y'see, and this stranger's was salt and pepper."

Sam reflexively turned to the painting behind her. The sallow man stared back, his salt-and-pepper hair an unkempt mess.

Then she remembered Brandon, the ranger she'd met on the trail, and the brisk, clipped note that had entered his voice when she'd told him about the stranger on her dock. *Brandon couldn't be the ranger Earnest met in the pub, could he?*

It made sense. Brandon hadn't told her about the figure he'd seen during the search—of course, he couldn't have—because it was just that: an obscure figure. His boss, the brisk lady at the ranger's office, probably would have told him he wasn't supposed to alarm the visitors. But it had worried him enough to give Sam his walkie-talkie. "*Better safe than sorry.*"

Sam wet her lips. "And so…uh…you think that Michael's ghost is hanging around the lake?"

"It's possible it's a ghost," Uncle Earnest said, clearly enjoying having a captivated listener. "But I think it's more likely a poltergeist. They're the stronger type of spirit, y'know? They can move stuff and throw stuff. They could even push you over the edge of a cliff, if they wanted to."

"Ah." Sam finally caught up with her new friend's mind. "You think he's killing the hikers."

"Absolutely," Earnest said. "Why else would so many hikers be going missing on the same trail? I'll bet Michael's body's lost in a gully somewhere, and when strangers pass by his resting place, he'll give them a shove or throw rocks at them or something, so that he'll not have to be alone anymore."

It's a ridiculous idea, Sam told herself, clenching her fists in her lap to stop their trembling. *Laughable, really.*

"Welp." Uncle Earnest sounded relaxed and a little sleepy. "I'd say it's about time to wrap up this radio program. Thanks for the chat, darlin'. It's always a pleasure to find someone equally interested in the supernatural. Call me up again another time, and I'll tell you about the giant panther that's currently plaguing Pleasantview."

"Sure thing," Sam said, trying to smile. "Thanks."

"Anytime, darlin'."

Sam turned off the radio. The fire had nearly eaten through its wood, so she added two new logs before sitting back in the chair and letting her thoughts consume her.

CHAPTER 11

SAM WOKE WITH A jolt. She wasn't in the plush armchair anymore, but was standing in front of the easel. Her left hand held a palette filled with swirls of well-blended paint, and her right was clasped around a paintbrush that barely touched the canvas.

She took a shaky breath and stepped back from the image. Though well painted, it shocked her deeply. *That came from me,* she realized, glancing at the vivid red paint soaked into her brush. *I created that.*

The man crouched on top of a shadowed, limp figure. His gray eyes, which were turned toward the painter, shone in the same way a wolf's did when it savored the blood of a freshly felled victim…which was exactly what the painting depicted. The man had a bloodied knife clenched between his teeth. Red ran over his lips and dripped off his chin. More blood coated the front of his gray flannel shirt and had smeared up to his elbows. He looked victorious, energized…and *ecstatic*, as though his whole reason for living centered on the gore dribbling over his tongue.

Sam felt as though she might be sick. She'd tried her hand at a lot of styles while practicing her art, but she'd never created anything so violent. She turned away, struggling to breathe.

More paintings stood propped against the furniture, all facing Sam. It was an onslaught of images: a shadowed shape barely visible between dense trees. The man, his pose stiff and somehow unnatural, stood at the end of the dock—*Peter's dock*—and watched the rippling water below. A single finger, detached from its hand, rested on the forest floor.

Sam couldn't bring herself to look at the rest. The paintings all showed frank, unrestrained violence. And the sallow, gray-eyed man loved it all.

Sam stumbled to the sink and gagged, but nothing came up. Her mind felt choked and frantic. She'd never dealt well with gore. She couldn't believe her subconscious was creating those scenes.

The fire spat, shaking Sam from her stupor, and she raised her head from the sink as she became aware of her surroundings.

The pot sat on the bench, empty except for the dregs of the minestrone soup. *Did I eat it while I was asleep?* Behind her, the fire crackled, having been fed recently. She must have tended to it for hours while she created the paintings. And to her left, a single empty mug stood on the bench, its handle directed toward the canvas.

First three, then two, now just one. It's almost like a countdown.

She couldn't stand looking at the paintings, so she moved through the room and turned each of them around. Including the four she'd created previously, there were nine in total. *Just how long did I spend painting?*

It was pitch-dark outside the window. Sam guessed it was somewhere between three and four in the morning, which meant it would be at least three hours until dawn showed over the tops of the mountains.

A bleating, wailing noise cut through the night air. Sam jumped and turned toward the door. *It's just an animal. We're in the middle of a forest, remember.*

The noise had sounded close—almost as though it had come from the lake. Sam had never heard a sound like that before; there had been something unnatural about the way it hung in the frosty air, almost as if it were filled with notes of grief.

I need more light.

Only one candle still burned, placed beside the canvas to provide light for her work. Between the nearly melted nub of wax and the fire, about half of the room was lit. Shadows filled the rest.

Peter left a flashlight, didn't he?

Sam opened the cupboard where she'd found the radio. Sitting near the back, beside a stack of spare batteries, was a large halogen flashlight. Sam turned it on. Its light, a brilliant white, was much cooler than the glow from the fire, and the beam cut through the darkness beautifully.

Sam crossed the room in five paces and undid the front door's latch. She was trembling, almost uncontrollably, as she nudged the wood and glanced outside.

The ground immediately in front of the cabin was empty, so Sam pressed the door open farther. The air stung her nose and cheeks. She raised the flashlight, passing it over the slope leading to the lake, then swung it across the shore in both directions. Mist had developed, but it wasn't yet thick enough to block her view. The shore was empty.

Sam turned the flashlight on the dock, and her heart fluttered like a trapped bird. At the end of the pier, clear in the flashlight's beam, knelt the man.

His back formed a severe curve as he sat on his haunches, hands clasped on the edge of the dock, and stared into the water. Sam thought he looked a little thicker than he did in the paintings, though it was hard to tell when he was hunched over. His hair was longer too; it hung around his face like a limp curtain.

The man's shoulders trembled, and his spine, deeply exaggerated, poked against his skin and dark shirt. Sam inhaled sharply, then clamped a hand over her mouth. No healthy human's back looked that desperately skeletal.

The man heard. He shouldn't have been able to at that distance, but he had. He swiveled his head to stare at Sam, and the light reflected off his eyes, making them glint like a cat's. Then he began to move, oddly, like an insect. Each limb twisted in an unnatural motion as he lurched forward, scuttling to the edge of the dock. Over the edge. *Under* the dock.

Sam collapsed to her knees as the scene branded itself into her mind. The man had lurched over the edge of the pier, reached one bizarrely long arm forward, and somehow grasped the underside of the wood. The rest of his body had followed smoothly, effortlessly, and he disappeared underneath, like a spider hiding from an intrusive stranger.

That's it, her mind gibbered. *I'm done. Hang the Heritage and hang Peter's generosity. I'm not staying a second longer.*

Sam sucked in a shaking breath and dashed into her cabin. She scrambled through the messy table until she found the car keys, then she ran back outside, waving her flashlight in erratic arcs to ward off the shadows. Her mind felt blank, as though it were incapable of processing what she'd just seen. All she cared about was getting to a road with actual streetlamps and houses. Her clothes and art supplies could stay in the cabin. *I'll come back for them another time, when it's broad daylight and I'm accompanied by the police or the FBI or whoever's in charge of dealing with weird stuff.*

The car was waiting for her in front of the shed. Sam skidded to a halt beside it and shone her flashlight through the windows to make sure the interior was empty then threw herself inside. She didn't realize how badly she was shaking until she slammed the door and found herself incapable of fitting the key into the ignition. Sam closed her eyes, leaned her forehead against the steering wheel, and took long, slow gulps of air. The viselike sensation around her chest gradually loosened as her nerves calmed, and she slotted the key into the ignition.

Good. Let's get the hell out of here.

Sam turned the key, but the motor failed to turn over. She bit at the inside of her cheek as fresh terror crawled up her spine.

"No," she muttered, trying to control her breathing, and turned the key again. Then a third, fourth, and fifth time. The car wouldn't start.

The motor's cold, that's all, she told herself, even though she knew it wasn't true. The car had never failed her before, not even when it snowed.

She tried again. The car's motor churned but failed to tick over. "Come on, come on, *come on.*"

Sam sat for a moment then turned her flashlight to the windows. The glass was fogging up, but she was alone as far as she could tell. She pressed the button to release the hood and scrambled out of the door, her heart thundering as she rounded the car to check its engine.

The problem was immediately obvious: someone had cut the fuel line—not just cut it, but cut it *twice*—and pulled the loose section of piping out to lay it neatly on top of the motor.

Someone doesn't want me to leave.

Instinct told her to turn off the flashlight, so she did. The only light came from the moon, which hung near one of the higher mountains, and the golden glow from inside the cabin.

Sam tried to calm her panicked mind and think through her options. Brandon would help her, she was sure, but the ranger's office was certainly closed at four in the morning. She had a two-way radio and codes to contact the police and emergency rescue team, though. They would take hours to reach her, but it was better than nothing.

Sam cast a final wary glance at the dock then began to slink toward the cabin. *I'll be safe inside at least. I can lock the door, and I'll have the ax, and—*

Motion inside the cabin made her freeze. There was a silhouette—a man's silhouette—barely visible in the window closest to the door. He swayed slightly as he faced the cabin's entrance. He must have gotten into her cabin while she struggled with the car, and he was waiting patiently. *Waiting for me.*

Panic boiled over into full-blown terror. Sam crept backward, toward the forest, keeping her body low and staying within the shed's shadows in case the man looked in her direction. When she reached the edge of the woods, she turned and ran.

CHAPTER 12

SAM'S LUNGS BURNED, AND every muscle in her legs ached as she forced herself up the incline at a blistering pace. Every few minutes, she paused and held her breath, listening to the forest for signs that she might have been followed. There were none. *Not so far.*

She'd had to choose between keeping to the paths or striking out into the woods. She would be harder to find in the forest, but also in greater danger of becoming lost and turning into another victim of Trail T-1. She kept to the paths.

Sam had no idea who, or *what*, had been inside the cabin, but she was certain she didn't want it following her. Whether Uncle Earnest had been right about the poltergeist or not, the thing in her cabin had almost certainly cut her fuel line and had been hiding in the corner of the room that would be hidden from view of anyone opening the door.

A flashlight in the dark night would stand out like a beacon, so Sam kept it off. The moonlight penetrated the trees in sparse splotches, offering just enough light to find her way. The light was not quite enough to save her shins from being barked and her arms from being snagged and scratched by the vines, though.

She rested only once, when she reached the clump of rocks halfway up the hill. She collapsed onto one of the stones and dragged in thick, sticky breaths as she listened to the forest; rustling trees, bats, insects, frogs, and even the occasional small mammal competed for her attention. She heard no human sounds, though, which she was immensely grateful for.

The ground looked lighter up ahead, and Sam pressed forward, ignoring the stitch in her side and the way sweat stuck her shirt to her body, despite the cold air. She pushed through another patch of weeds and finally broke onto the main path. *Trail T-1.*

She turned right, toward the clearing that held the map. The ranger's office wouldn't be open, but Sam was banking on the idea that her stalker wouldn't expect her to go there, and she could wait by the front door for the morning shift to arrive. *It's not that far from dawn anyway. This'll be fine. We'll be fine.*

Sam half walked, half jogged down the trail. It felt endless. Just when she was beginning to panic that she'd taken a bad turn and was on a completely wrong path, she nearly tripped over the chain barrier. She let her breath out in a hoarse cheer and ducked under the blockade.

Visibility was much better in the clearing. She increased her speed, ignoring her aching legs and thundering heart in her eagerness to reach the sign.

"Okay," Sam whispered, turning her light to examine the large map. "Okay, this is good. We're good. Let's find the ranger's office and get out of this place."

She started with the You Are Here tag and circled out. She found landmarks, lookouts, and intersections, but not the office. Sam's heart dropped as her circles became wider and wider.

"Damn it, where are you?"

She turned her flashlight toward the symbols key in the map's corner. A tree shape represented noteworthy plants, a sun hovering over a ledge was for lookouts, and exclamation points indicated difficult sections. Nothing for the ranger's office.

"No, no, no, *no, no.*"

Sam took a step back and turned her light across the board again. *It's got to be somewhere!*

Then she saw it: a note at the base of the map, written in neat cursive.

Need emergency help? Rangers patrol these woods during the day. The park office is located at the entrance to the park, on the corner of Harob Forest Road and Mindy Lane.

"The entrance to the park..."

Sam slumped against the sign and cradled her head in her

hands. The entrance was a full two hours' drive away. *How long would it take me to walk?*

If she'd brought her walkie-talkie, she'd have been able to call for help. But of course, she hadn't; she'd left it nestled among her art supplies in the cabin, which was playing host to a stranger.

And it wasn't just the walkie-talkie that was missing. She was desperately thirsty but had no water. More, she wore only her light jacket, and the night chill was seeping through the thin fabric, making her shiver. It would get worse closer to dawn.

I've got no choice except to return to the cabin…or freeze to death in the forest.

She sat for a moment, basking in the noises of the night. Tears leaked out of the corners of her eyes, but she didn't brush them away. Instead, she pulled herself to her feet, swallowed the metallic taste that had developed in her mouth, and turned to the cordoned-off trail.

"You've got to be strong, Sammy," her mother had whispered during those last few hours on her deathbed. Her voice had rasped horribly as her eyes stared, unfocused, at the off-white ceiling. Sam had squeezed her hand, but her mother didn't seem to feel it. *"You're going to have to face a lot of things without me. Be strong, like I know you are. Be brave."*

"Be strong," Sam echoed, forcing her feet to move her body onto the trail leading to the dock, the sabotaged car, and the *thing* waiting for her. "Be brave."

CHAPTER 13

THIRST BECAME AN INCREASINGLY pressing issue as Sam retraced her path through the woods. She tried to ignore it, but the hike had left her mouth dry, and her head was starting to pound.

I should be passing the rock slide soon. Then it's just another hour—or a bit more—to the cabin. And maybe the thing inside the cabin's moved on by now. Maybe it'll be safe again.

She stumbled over branches and rocks, staggered through a clump of vines, and hesitated. *I don't remember the path being this choked on the way up. I haven't taken a wrong turn, have I?*

Sam paused and turned in a semicircle. Nothing looked familiar…not that unfamiliarity meant anything. She wouldn't have recognized anything except major landmarks, and there weren't many of those in her part of the forest. The path definitely seemed narrower and more cluttered than she remembered it, though.

Keep calm, Sam told herself as anxiety began to rise in her. *This whole place is like a giant bowl. As long as you're walking downhill, you'll reach the lake eventually, then you can just follow the beach until you find the cabin.*

She wasn't sure if she was imagining it or not, but she thought the sky was in the early stages of dawn. There was definitely some sort of light ahead, at least.

Wait…that's not natural light.

Sam squinted through the trees at the faint, flickering glow. *Is it the cabin? Did I find my way back by accident?* Her heart rose for a second before she tamped down the excitement. *No, that's impossible. I'm still a long way from the beach.*

And yet, something was glowing through the trees like a beacon. Sam moved forward, fighting through the tangled growth, and found herself in a clearing.

Ahead stood a cabin. It was worlds away from the tidy, orderly house Peter had lent her. Squat and dark, it looked as though it had been constructed by hand, then repeatedly repaired and patched as it slowly broke down. A tarpaulin was strapped over one side of the roof, and the windows had no glass.

Behind the cabin, in a tangled vegetable patch, weeds fought the tomato plants for dominance. Beyond that was a makeshift hutch that, judging by the faint clucking sounds, housed fowl. The light Sam had seen was coming from the cabin's window, where a single candle flickered on the sill.

Prudence told her to turn around and disappear back into the forest. Necessity, though, was far more insistent. *If there's a house, there'll be water.*

Sam hesitated for just a second before stepping out from the shadows of the trees. She didn't like the cabin's appearance, but it seemed empty, and she was in no position to reject a chance to drink. *Especially if I'm lost. I have no idea how long it might take me to get back to the lake.*

One of the fowl fluttered inside the enclosure, and Sam jumped. The bird didn't look like any sort of domestic hen or duck, so Sam guessed it might be a wild bird.

Who could possibly live here? They can't have permission from the government, surely, or they would have built their cabin by the lake like Peter did. It couldn't be someone on the run from the law, could it? Or…is it related to that thing at the lake?

Sam approached the door. She was almost completely certain the cabin was empty, but that didn't stop her from calling, "Hello?"

Only the very faint ticking of a clock answered.

Sam glanced behind herself, where the clearing was still and dark, and then, ignoring the anxious palpitations in her chest, she pushed on the cabin's door.

The cabin's single room looked a lot like the outside: well used and slowly falling apart. A layer of compact dirt covered the floor. The furniture—a table, a single chair, and a large collection of oddly shaped shelves—appeared hand-made and took up most of the room. A brick fireplace stood in the corner. Unlike Peter's fireplace, it was small, grimy, and looked frequently used.

Trinkets and knickknacks covered the shelves, ranging from compasses and maps to melamine bowls, crockery, a mug that smelled faintly of whiskey, an old-fashioned clock, and a stack of mismatched cloths.

Sparkling silver caught Sam's attention, and she turned to see a board hung above the table. Two dozen nails had been crudely hammered into the wood, and from each one hung a knife.

Some were small—just paring knives, no larger than the ones Peter kept in his kitchen drawers—but others were long and serrated. Two were butcher knives. The bench below them was stained red.

Nausea grew in Sam's stomach. She staggered backward and bumped into something leaning against the wall; turning, she saw a row of axes and a chain saw.

Calm down, Sam told herself, as cold sweat built across her body. *This house belongs to someone living in the woods. Of course he'd have to catch and kill his own food. It's nothing abnormal.*

There're so many knives, though. At least twenty. Surely one person doesn't need twenty.

Sam squeezed her hands into fists as she rotated on the spot. The anxious feeling in her chest was exploding into terror.

"Calm down, calm down, calm down," she muttered to herself, willing her mind to unfreeze. "Just find the water and get out."

There was no kitchen, tap, or sink. A large bowl sat on the bench, half-filled with liquid, but Sam cringed away from it. She had no idea if it was drinking water, used for bathing, or something else.

There's got to be clean water somewhere.

A cupboard near the fireplace caught her eye. It was the only storage unit with doors, which made it look like a kitchen pantry. Sam pulled open the doors.

Unlabeled bottles crowded the shelves. Some looked as though they were full of jams. Others seemed to contain pickled vegetables. Two held some type of dried meat jerky, and others were full of a brown-tinted liquid that she suspected was alcohol. Behind everything else was a stack of water bottles.

There were close to fifty of them. Most of the seals were broken, and they had clearly been refilled multiple times, but Sam spotted a small cluster of unopened bottles near the back and took one.

She pushed the rest of the jars back into place and reached for the cupboard's handles to close the doors, but she hesitated. Another row of containers stood on the highest shelf, lined up far more neatly then the bottles below them. They each had one small, long item floating in clear liquid.

Curiosity got the better of Sam. She shoved the bottle of water into her jacket pocket then took one of the jars.

Floating inside, gently bouncing off the glass walls, was a woman's finger.

A horrified gurgle escaped Sam's throat, and she shoved the container back onto the shelf. The jars each held a single finger. All index fingers. All from different hands.

She couldn't tear her eyes away from the horrific sight. There were so many types of fingers—slender and feminine, gnarled, stubbly, or wrinkled—all preserved with care.

Sounds filtered through Sam's panic, and she became aware of leaves crunching and twigs snapping as someone moved through the forest. Sam turned toward the window that overlooked the path she'd come down.

It looks familiar, somehow…

Fresh adrenaline shot through her as she recognized the scene. She was horribly familiar with the sick, twisted trees lining the dirt path. *It's the image from my painting. Any second, the gray-eyed man's going to come into view, carrying an ax as he returns home—*

A figure was materializing out of the darkness, catching faint glints of moonlight as he moved into view. Sam shrunk away from the window, barely daring to breathe as she searched for an escape. The door faced the man's path, making it impossible to slip outside without attracting his attention. But there was nowhere to hide inside the one-room cabin.

The footsteps grew closer. Sam's eyes landed on the window at the opposite side of the room, and seizing the only option available to her, she clambered onto the bloodied bench and slid over the sill.

She misjudged the size of the window and fell into the bushes outside with a muffled *whump*. She thought the footsteps paused for a moment, as though the man had heard her. Then his pace increased, and the cabin's door was pulled open.

Sam tried to shrink into a ball and squeezed her eyes closed, hoping the spindly bushes would conceal her. She heard the man walk through his cabin, slowly and ponderously, then come to a halt not far from the window.

A horrible realization hit Sam, and her stomach dropped. *I didn't close the cupboard doors.*

The cabin's entrance opened with a bang. Sam shrunk farther into the bushes, aware that their patchy branches did a poor job of masking her. The footsteps drew closer, coming down the side of the cabin, and Sam held her breath, squeezing her shaking hands into fists, as her stalker rounded the house and came into view.

The moonlight hit his face as he paused barely ten feet from her hiding spot, and she saw the familiar gray eyes, the salt-and-pepper stubble, and the vicious, healing scar on his cheek.

Just like in the paintings. They're so accurate that I could have been creating them from a photo.

The man scanned the woods behind his cabin. Sam didn't dare inhale, even though her lungs ached and her head throbbed. Her heartbeat was loud in her ears, and she felt certain that the man would be able to hear it. He wasn't looking in her direction, though, but faced the forest. Sam caught a brief glimpse of an ax—*Uncle Peter's ax*—clasped in his hand before the man stepped toward the trees and disappeared between them with unexpected litheness.

CHAPTER 14

SAM DIDN'T MOVE FOR a long time. Her heart beat frantically, and she struggled to draw breath. Even though the forest was still, she kept imagining she heard footsteps heralding the man's return.

Gotta get moving, Sam. Get to your feet. Get away from his house.

Movement seemed impossible, though. Her limbs were locked up with terror, and her body couldn't draw in oxygen quickly enough. Then a fat, heavy insect landed on Sam's face and broke the trance. She jolted to her feet, fighting her way out from the bushes, and staggered through the clearing. One of the fowls squawked in alarm as she passed the hutch. Sam glanced behind herself once, searching between the trees, but the only movement came from the trembling leaves. She turned toward the woods that would lead in the direction opposite to the way the man had taken.

Terror had given her strength, and Sam ran as quickly and as silently as the dense woods would allow her to. She didn't dare turn her flashlight back on. Instead, she held both hands ahead of herself to protect her face from the worst of the scratching branches and focused on moving her feet in long, careful strides. She didn't know which direction she was going, but she didn't care. All she wanted was to be away from the strange cabin and away from the man, to keep him from adding any of her fingers to his sick collection.

The woods cleared, and Sam stumbled to a halt on the edge of a drop-off. Her legs were weak, and her lungs ached, so she let herself slump onto the rocks to rest. Dehydration taxed her body, setting up a pounding headache behind her eyes. Remembering she'd pocketed the bottle of water, Sam felt for it in her jacket. To her surprise and relief, the bottle had survived her fall out of the window. She tugged the cap off and drained it.

Dawn was still at least half an hour away, and the moon bathed the area in its pale light. Trees coated the slope ahead of Sam, which dipped until it met the lake. Dense fog hid the water from sight. Sam thought she saw a faint glow on the beach. *Peter's cabin. Should I be going back there?*

I don't think I have a choice.

As soon as she'd stopped moving, the cold had begun biting at her in earnest. She didn't have nearly enough layers, and she knew the temperature would continue to drop until dawn broke.

Besides, there's the radio in the cabin. If I go inside for just a minute to grab the radio, the codes, some water, and my heavier jacket, at least I'll have a proper chance of getting out of here.

With any luck, Sam thought, the man would either still be

searching the woods or have returned to his cabin to check that nothing had been stolen. Sam didn't think he would wait for her in Peter's house a second time.

She crumpled the empty water bottle and tucked it inside her pocket before climbing to her aching legs. She'd found her way to one of the steeper parts of the mountain and had to slow to a crawl to climb down the cliffs to the shore.

A hint of light dissolved the stars near the opposite side of the lake as the sun started its daily climb over the mountain ridge. The cold increased as Sam moved lower. By the time she stumbled onto the beach, uncontrollable shivers wracked her. She didn't dare remove her hands from where she'd tucked them inside her jacket, even though the condensed fog dripped from her nose. The cabin's fire, burned down to embers, provided a faint glow to guide her to the cabin.

Sam slowed her pace as she drew closer, glancing between the dock and the cabin. It was hard to see through the mist, but both seemed deserted. Sam was too close to exhaustion to give the situation as much caution as she knew it deserved, and she only paused to glance through the cabin's window and check the room was empty before pushing inside.

The difference in temperature was amazing, and Sam sucked a deep breath of warm air into her lungs. She knew she couldn't stay long, but she dared to take a moment to hold her icy fingers over the embers.

As she warmed her hands, Sam took a quick assessment of the cabin. The paintings were exactly where she'd left them, facing the walls. The ax was missing from beside the fireplace, though, and Sam didn't like the way that made her feel.

The cabin seemed still and quiet. As soon as feeling returned to her fingers, Sam went to the kitchen sink and took one of the small paring knives out of the drawer then moved to the cupboard to get the radio.

"What..."

The radio was also gone. Sam glanced around the room, hoping she'd forgotten to put it away, but it was missing. *No, not missing. Taken. He wanted me to be completely stranded. No car, no phone, no radio...*

"The walkie-talkie!"

Sam crossed to the table. Its surface was covered with papers and art supplies, and Sam dug through them until she found the black box hidden near the back, where she'd tossed it after the less-than-helpful talk with the female ranger. Sam tried to guess the time; judging by the light that was bleeding across the outside sky, it had to be after six but before seven. *What time do the rangers come in?*

She pressed the button and said, "Hello?"

A prolonged crackle answered her, then a click and a man's voice, sounding half-asleep, replied, "Yeah, hello, this is the ranger's office. How can I be of assistance?"

Sam closed her eyes and drew in a relieved breath. The voice was familiar. She pressed the button again and tried to keep her hands from shaking. "Hi, this is Sam. I'm staying at the cabin by the lake. A strange man's stalking me, and I think he might be responsible for the missing hikers."

CHAPTER 15

"SAM!" A SHARP NOTE filled the voice, cutting through its tiredness. "This is Brandon. We met the other day. Tell me exactly what happened."

Sam did, in stumbling and confused fragments. The panicky, sleepless night was catching up to her. She knew she wasn't making as much sense as she should have, but Brandon interrupted only twice, to clarify the order of events. She told him about her car cables being cut, seeing a figure inside her cabin, and discovering the shanty in the woods. She expected him to laugh at the part where she'd found the fingers preserved in jars, but he didn't. The only part of the story Sam didn't share was seeing the figure at the end of the dock. *That's too fantastical for anyone to believe.*

When Sam finished, she held her breath and waited for Brandon's response. He didn't say anything for a moment, and she tried to imagine his face. *Is he laughing at me? Does he think it's a prank, maybe, or that I'm delusional?*

But then he spoke, and her fears melted away. He sounded anxious, but maintained a well-practiced note of authority in his voice. "Sam, are you somewhere safe?"

"Uh…I think so." Sam glanced around the cabin. She hadn't searched the upstairs room, but it had been completely silent since her arrival. "I'm in the cabin."

"Have you locked the door?"

Sam crossed the room and pulled the bolt. "I have now."

"Do you have a weapon?"

"I've got a small knife."

"That's better than nothing," Brandon said. "Sam, the first thing I want you to do is ensure you're safe. Search the cabin. I'm going to drive down there to pick you up. It'll take a bit over an hour, so the priority right now is to make sure you're not in danger."

Sam was already moving through the cabin, searching in any and every crevice a human could possibly fit. She opened each of the downstairs cupboards then moved upstairs, walkie-talkie in one hand and knife in the other, to search the bedroom. It was empty.

"Okay, I'm definitely alone."

"Good. Keep the door locked, and make sure you've got the knife and walkie-talkie with you at all times. I'm on my way, but if you see or hear anything, let me know immediately."

"Will do."

"See you soon, Sam."

The line went quiet, and Sam released a long breath. She approached the doors overlooking the balcony and gazed through the glass windows.

The sun had finally breached the top of the mountains and begun to spread its glow across the lake. The mist was still dense but seemed to be clearing.

Sam weighed her options. Brandon seemed to think she should stay in the cabin. On one hand, it was at least somewhat defensible. On the other, it would be easy for the gray-eyed man to find her there.

She took the stairs back to the ground floor and gazed at the paintings propped against the furniture and walls.

There was so much she didn't understand. Why had she been painting the images? How had she known the man's face before ever seeing it? She knew there were clues somewhere, possibly even hidden in the images, but she was just being too obtuse to notice them.

She didn't want to look at the paintings again, but a desperate need to *understand* compelled her to turn them around one at a time.

First was the painting of the man standing on the crop of rocks overlooking the lake. It was a replica of what she'd seen while on the lake, though she didn't know how her asleep self had guessed his face. The second painting was of water, swirling and frantic— another echo of her canoeing experience. *At least, I think it is. I fell into weedy, muddy water, but the painting is clear and blue.*

She turned over the third image and grimaced at the sight

of the man crouched over his victim, blood dripping down his chin from the knife he'd clasped between his teeth. The one after that depicted a single bloodied finger lying among the leaves. *Almost like I'd known what he did to his victims. But that should be impossible.*

Next was a glimpse of the man between dense trees then one of him running toward the viewer, a long, serrated knife gripped in his fist, a vicious smile spread across his face.

Following that, she turned the painting of the gray-eyed man striding down the path leading to his home. Again, Sam had to face the idea that her mind had been showing her images before they'd happened. The appearance of the gnarled, sickened trees lining the path, the ax clasped in his hand, and even the way he looked—only faintly visible among the shadows—were true to Sam's experience just hours before.

Then she turned another painting, one she hadn't looked at the day before, and saw a bottle of clear liquid with a woman's finger floating in it. Sam's stomach flipped, and she looked away.

After that came the first image she'd created: the close-up of the man's face. The salt-and-pepper hair, the stubble, the gray eyes, and the red scar on his cheek were all so familiar. She'd thought when she'd first seen it that it was a face she'd known before—but she was no closer to remembering from where.

The final painting showed the man standing on the edge of the dock, watching the water intently. Sam found herself trans-fixed by it. She felt that if she could only see what the gray-eyed man was seeing, she would have answers.

There's something in the water he can't stay away from. He's been coming back to the cabin almost every day since I've been here, just to look into the lake.

Sam remembered the way he'd crawled over the edge of the dock, moving to hide underneath it like a giant insect, and couldn't stop shudders from creeping down her spine. *That wasn't human. No way, no how. Does that mean Uncle Earnest was right? Is he some sort of vengeful spirit? A poltergeist?*

She thought back to the cabin, with its bottles of water, jars of food, vegetable garden, and poultry—all things a human needed.

And yet...I couldn't have imagined seeing him crawl under the dock, could I? I'd not long woken up from a concussion, but even so, it was too clear and too real to be a hallucination. If only I could look over the edge...if only I could see...

Sam had walked toward the front door without realizing it, and she stopped herself with one hand on the bolt. She shook her head, trying to dispel the tiredness that was fogging her mind.

Nope. No. Definitely not. We're not going outside. We're not setting so much as a toe on that dock. It would be insanity.

Sam turned back to the room. The paintings surrounded her, smothering her in their portent. Her eyes fell on the image of the man leaning over the dock and watching the water. He looked so focused—obsessed, even.

It's too cold to stay outdoors for long, so the man probably won't come back until later today, if at all. And Brandon will be here in an hour. This could be my only chance to see what he sees. To understand.

"What the hell," Sam said, and unbolted the door. "It's hardly the craziest thing I've done this week."

She paused on the threshold and gazed up and down the length of the shore. The canoe, empty, still rested on the dirt, one end barely dipped into the water. The mountain's trees rippled as a breeze tugged at their branches. The mist was gone. Dark clouds clustered over the sky, threatening rain. The cold air bit at Sam's nose and cheeks, but it no longer had the cruel edge she'd felt when walking home.

Sam closed the door behind herself and moved toward the dock. Its supports, still damp from the mist, stood out against the crystalline water. Hyperaware, she approached the lake. Every birdcall and rustle of the tree branches seemed to hold potential danger, and Sam kept her eyes roving over her surroundings. Instead of stepping onto the dock, she followed the ground's gentle slope until the edge of the lake lapped at her sneakers, then knelt to look under the pier.

There were no dark, hulking shapes lurking underneath or glowing red eyes watching her. Sam let her breath out, swallowed the lump in her throat, and moved back until she could climb onto the dock. The first slat creaked under her feet, and she hesitated.

Don't chicken out now. This is what you wanted, isn't it?

Sam narrowed her eyes, squared her shoulders, and began to move down the dock, testing each step before she dared place her weight on it. Her breath caught every time the wood groaned.

Her limbs were trembling by the time she reached the dock's

end, and she lowered herself to her knees, one hand on the support. She couldn't stop herself from imagining how she must look from the shore; crouched over the end of the dock, she would be an almost perfect replica of the man who'd haunted her stay at the lake.

Shaking fingers gripped the edge of the wood as Sam leaned forward, extending her torso over the lip of the dock, to look into the water below.

CHAPTER 16

AT FIRST, SHE SAW only her own reflection, her anxiety-widened eyes set in pale skin. Then she looked past the water's surface and saw what had captivated the man so much.

"Oh," Sam said simply, as revulsion and horror rose through her chest and threatened to choke her.

Suspended in the water, only a foot below the surface, floated a man's body. The white face was turned toward her, its empty eye sockets staring blindly. Sam could see into the open mouth: the tongue was gone—devoured—and white teeth poked out of shrunken gums. The corpse's skin was frayed and pocked with holes where decay and water creatures had eaten through the flesh. Shoulder-length bronze hair washed around the head, making a gently swaying halo.

Sam felt frozen in place, unable to release her grip on the edge of the dock and incapable of looking away. The body's limbs were intact; its limp arms were spread out and had become tangled in the thick weeds. Her eyes turned to the figure's right hand, which was missing a finger.

A strangled, horrified noise escaped Sam's throat. She wrenched herself backward, away from the body in the water, and stumbled upright. Her chest had constricted, and panic set her fingers shaking. She turned and began running toward the shore.

One of the dock's beams splintered under her feet, and Sam threw herself forward to avoid falling through the hole. She hit the dock hard, knocking the wind out of her lungs, and her vision swam.

She rolled onto her back, trying to smother the groans of fear and pain that escaped between her clenched teeth, and looked toward the end of the dock.

A pale hand stretched up, over the lip of the pier, and slapped onto the wooden edge, sending a spray of water ahead of it. Sam opened her mouth to scream, but the sound died as a gurgle in her throat. A second hand emerged from the water, reaching forward and smacking onto the wood in front of the first, and then the muscles in the arms flexed as they began pulling the body out of the lake.

The head emerged, raining water, its empty eye sockets focused on Sam, its mouth open to expose the rotting gums and white teeth.

Sam turned and threw herself down the dock, no longer caring if the wood gave out under her feet. She could hear the cadaver dragging itself onto the dock. Its nails scratched at the wood. The water that dripped from it made quiet tapping noises. Then the being exhaled, expelling the liquid from its lungs, and drew a raspy, laborious breath.

Sam reached the end of the dock and turned toward the cabin, adrenaline powering her aching legs, her lungs fighting to bring in enough oxygen to support the exertion. She didn't stop moving until her hands had fixed around the cabin's metal door handle and wrenched it open.

She turned on the cabin's threshold, prepared to slam the door if the horror had followed her, but the dock was empty.

"What…*what on earth…*"

Sam clung to the wooden doorframe, her eyes scanning the shore, the trees, the dock, and the lake. Struggling to draw breath, she felt dizzy and nauseated, and her head throbbed. She didn't think her legs would hold her weight for much longer. No shapes appeared out of the water, so she closed and bolted the door.

There are two men, Sam realized with sickening horror. *I've been trying to hide from a single person, but there are actually two of them. The gray-eyed man and…*that.

It was mercifully quiet inside the cabin. Sam cast a glance at the paintings spaced around the room, then she grabbed the walkie-talkie from the table and stumbled toward the stairs. *The bedroom's balcony has the best view out of anywhere in the cabin.*

Sam's body felt leaden as she climbed the stairs. When she reached the bedroom, she opened the balcony doors and settled on the edge of the bed, which was close enough to the balcony to allow her to watch the dock.

How long until Brandon gets here? Forty minutes? Half an hour?

Sam rubbed at her aching eyes. Everything hurt, from her pounding head to her dry mouth to her shaking legs. *At least it's warmer in the cabin's upper level.* Sam scooted farther back onto the bed and pulled the quilt around herself. It was soft, familiar, and safe, and she sighed as she nestled into it.

The minutes ticked by slowly as she stared out over the balcony, her eyes fixed on the dark pier, and the tension gradually left her limbs. As the immediate edge of panic faded, exhaustion set in; she'd barely slept the previous night, and she was drained both physically and emotionally. She felt dazed and dull. The birdcalls filtering through the open balcony doors were pleasantly repetitive and comforting. She watched as the last shreds of mist dissipated, leaving the lake clear and smooth. The sky was starting to darken with heavy clouds, though. *We might be in for some rain later today.*

Sam didn't even realize her eyes were closing until she found herself falling backward onto the bed, and by then it was too late to fight.

Her dream was rushed and indistinct. She saw herself painting. She was frantic with stress as she held a jar in one hand and copied its contents onto the canvas. Inside the jar was a finger...*no, not just anyone's finger—my finger.* The gray-eyed man owned it, and she had to paint it quickly, before he took it back, so she would never forget what it looked like. She couldn't get it right, though, and the people behind her were becoming agitated. They begged her to hurry. She was supposed to paint their fingers next, and they'd already been waiting such a long time. *Denzel will never forgive me if I don't deliver the fingers to the Heritage in time…*

Sam snapped awake, and her body revolted against the abruptly interrupted sleep cycle. She couldn't immediately tell what had disturbed her. She was still on the bed, wrapped in the quilt. The sky was clogged with dark clouds, and the balcony doors stood open, letting the chilled air in, though she didn't feel cold.

Then she became aware of the body behind her. It seemed so natural, lying beside her on the bed, its chest pressed to her back and its arm draped over her waist like a lover's.

But he wasn't alive. *Not anymore.*

He felt familiar, Sam realized, because she'd already met him. They'd been companions for days. He was the mind that had guided her hand while she slept, funneling his memories into the paintings she'd so skillfully created. He'd taught her to recognize the gray-eyed man's face and shown her the deaths. He'd led her to set up the mugs as a crude countdown. And his was the figure she'd seen knelt on the edge of the dock, staring into the water day after day, as he watched over his final resting place.

Sam didn't dare move. He felt so human and yet so *cold*, as he lay behind her, embracing her. It almost felt *normal*. Slowly, cautiously, Sam turned her head to look over her shoulder.

The two empty eye sockets stared back. His brow, where white bone peeked through the gaps in the flesh, was creased in concern for her. His lips opened then, and his voice was dry, raspy, and urgent.

"He's coming," the cadaver whispered. "Run."

CHAPTER 17

SAM LAUNCHED HERSELF OUT of the bed, a scream held at bay behind tightly squeezed lips. She hit the cabin's wall and turned to face the bed.

The corpse was gone.

Sam gasped. Her heart thundered as she rubbed her sweaty palms across her jeans. *A dream. It was just a dream. Calm down.*

And yet, there was a strange smell about the room, like dirty water and organic decay. It felt thick in Sam's lungs and was somehow familiar.

Sam swore under her breath. She snatched the walkie-talkie off the bedside table and pressed the button. "Brandon, are you there? It's Sam."

The crackling static answered her. Sam waited for nearly a full minute then pressed the button again. "Brandon? Hello?"

She listened with increasing frustration to the background

noise then paced to the balcony and looked outside. The sky was still dark and swirling, creating strange patterns on the water's surface. Sam tried to guess the time, but that was nearly impossible without the sun.

Then she heard the faint click of a closing door. Sam's heart froze, and she turned toward the stairs leading to the ground floor. She raised the walkie-talkie to her mouth and pressed the button.

"Brandon?" She didn't dare raise her voice above a whisper. "Please, please answer me. He's here."

The only reply was static.

Footsteps echoed through the floor below then stopped. Sam imagined the man standing in the center of the room, his gray eyes scanning the myriad paintings depicting him. *Would they confuse him? Disturb him, even?* Then the footsteps resumed, leading across the room and toward the stairwell.

Panic flooded her, lending her tired limbs strength. Sam cast around for some type of defense. She'd left the knife in the downstairs room, and there was no other weapon in the bedroom. *Nowhere to hide, either.*

The footsteps changed timbre as he began climbing the stairs. Sam clamped both hands over her mouth, trying to muffle her frantic breathing, as she searched with increasing desperation for some kind of rescue. Her eyes landed on the window.

Sam crossed to the balcony's banister and looked over the edge. She hated how far away the ground seemed, but there was no time left to find any other option. She swung her leg over the wooden barrier, and her heart jumped as the wood swayed under her weight. The footsteps were nearly at the top of the stairs.

There's no time. Do it now!

She dropped over the outside of the banister and lowered herself until her hands clung to the wooden struts and her legs dangled over the drop.

The man appeared at the top of the stairs. His wild, steel-gray eyes fixed on Sam for a split second before she let go.

Impact forced Sam's breath from her as she hit the ground. Pain shot up her right leg, and for a moment of blind panic, she thought she might have broken it. It still moved, though, and could take enough weight to let her scramble on her back away from the foot of the cabin.

The man stood on the balcony, his bony hands gripping the rail she'd just released. Sam hadn't realized before just how tall he was; he seemed to fill the entire doorway, and sinewy muscles bulged under his dirty shirt. He had a rope coil slung around one shoulder, and she thought she saw the edge of the ax under his dark moleskin coat.

Sam stared, transfixed, at the furious gray eyes that had haunted her. *They seem so much more malevolent in the flesh.*

The man's lip curled into a sneer, and he turned back to the room. He wasn't reckless or desperate enough to follow her over the banister, which meant the climb down the stairs would buy Sam a few seconds.

A few seconds for what? My car won't start, and there's not enough time to hide.

Sam scrambled to her feet, wincing as pain flashed up her injured leg. She turned in a semicircle, searching for an escape, and caught sight of a dark car parked twenty meters away, near the path that led toward the entrance to the park. Its driver door stood open.

Did the gray-eyed man drive here? I didn't see a car on his property, but that doesn't mean he didn't have one. If he left the keys in the ignition...

No matter how repulsive she found the idea of touching his property, Sam knew she couldn't reject the only lifeline offered to her. She made for the car as quickly as she could, gritting her teeth against the pain stabbing through her leg.

She'd nearly reached the vehicle when she caught sight of the emblem emblazoned on the door. *Harob Park Ranger's Office.*

"Brandon..." Sam threw herself toward the driver's side.

The ranger lay slumped across the steering wheel, one hand thrown over the dash, the other lying limply in his lap. His face was turned toward the door as his dark eyes gazed sightlessly out of ashen skin and his mouth hung open in an expression of surprise.

"Brandon!" Sam pulled open the door and shook the ranger's arm. He slid a few inches sideways before catching in his locked seat belt. Something dark protruded from his back. Sam's hands fluttered toward it, but she couldn't bring herself to touch the knife embedded between the man's shoulder blades. "No, no, no, please, no—"

She turned to face the cabin, forest, and lake as she fought to

101

draw breath. She couldn't see the man. *Is he still inside the cabin? In the woods? Why hasn't he followed me?*

The answer came easily. *I have no way to escape. He knows he can take his time stalking me. That's what this is for him—a hunt… and he doesn't want it to end too quickly.*

Sam turned back to the car and brushed Brandon's chocolate hair away from his face with shaking fingers. A sob stuck in her throat, but she pushed it back down and blinked to clear her eyes. *Focus. Find a way out.*

Sam looked in the ignition, hoping it might still hold the keys, but the man had taken them. She then leaned over Brandon's shoulder to look into the back seat.

A first-aid kit, an animal trap, a thick guidebook, spare boots, and a jacket were scattered about the back. If Brandon had brought any weapons, the man had taken them. A blanket lay crumpled on the car's floor behind the driver's seat, and Sam stared at it. That morning's events were slowly falling into place.

Brandon had said it would take him an hour to reach Sam, but the ranger's office was more than two hours away, at the entrance to the park. That meant he must have already been in the forest when Sam contacted him. He'd probably been checking the park's traps for animals to tag and monitor, if the cage in the back of the car was any indication.

Is it possible the gray-eyed man had a walkie-talkie? Or had he been near enough to Brandon to listen in on our conversation? If he'd heard us, and if he'd gotten to the car before Brandon did, it would have been all too easy to hide under the blanket in the back seat. He'd have an easy ride to the cabin before attacking his unknowing host.

Sam squeezed her eyes closed, fighting her grief and fear, and stepped back from the car. A spot of rain hit her arm. She turned in a semicircle, fruitlessly searching for the man. *He'll be somewhere he can watch me without being seen. He wants to see what I'm going to do. What* am *I going to do? I could go into the cabin and get one of the paring knives out of the drawer…as though that would be any sort of defense against an ax. Or I could go into the forest and try to outrun him…but I'd have nowhere to go, and he's more familiar with the woods than I am. Or…*

Sam's eyes landed on the canoe, its tip barely dipped into the water. *There aren't any other boats. If I got onto the lake, he wouldn't be able to follow me.*

Thunder cracked overhead. Sam ran, moving her pained leg as fast as she could, toward the water's edge. She didn't let herself think about what she would do once she was on the water or how she hoped to escape from the forest; everything else was secondary to her immediate need to put as much distance as she could between herself and her stalker.

Sam was nearly at the canoe when the man burst from the forest's edge. He kept his body low and moved lithely as he arced toward her. She caught a glimpse of his eyes, manic with excitement, his hungry smile stretching the scar across his cheek. Then Sam's hands hit the canoe's end, and she shoved it into the water with all of her strength.

It was heavy and ground forward slowly. Sam poured every bit of adrenaline into the task, fighting against gravity and the boat, until it was waterborne and rushing across the lake's surface. Sam continued pushing it until the water reached her thighs, then hauled herself over the edge of the canoe. It nearly overbalanced, but Sam threw herself toward its opposite side to right it, then grabbed the paddle and plunged it into the water.

She glanced over her shoulder and saw that the man had paused on the edge of the lake. He held his head high, and a cruel delight stretched his lips into a grin.

Sam pulled the paddle through the water, and the canoe spun. She quickly changed sides, trying to temper her frantic energy to a more efficient level. She didn't dare look behind herself again, but she could hear the man moving; the dirt crunched under his boots as he paced along the shore. He was moving languidly—*confidently*—and Sam didn't like it. She focused on drawing her paddle through the water, moving the canoe farther into the lake. Farther from *him*.

Thunder crashed again, and what had been gentle spits of water turned into a downpour.

The footsteps changed from a crunching noise to a quiet thud, accompanied by a strange scraping sound. Sam couldn't stop herself from looking, and ice-cold fear ran through her chest. The man was pacing down the length of the dock. He'd taken the rope off his shoulder, and a large grappling hook hung from its end, its edges viciously sharp. He let the metal hook drag along the slats to create the scraping sound that had set Sam's teeth on edge.

He thought I might use the canoe, and he came prepared.

Sam swore and pulled her paddle through the water too quickly, breaking the canoe's momentum and sending it into a spin. A muted whirring noise replaced the scraping. Sam moved the paddle to the other side of the boat but overcompensated again, and her vessel lurched. Before she could correct it, a loud *clang* filled her ears, and she felt the boat rock as the grappling hook found its mark.

Sam turned to see the hook had landed inside the boat but hadn't yet caught on the wood. Pure instinct took over and pushed her to fight. She dived toward the hook, intending to lift it and throw it overboard, but just as her hand tightened around the cold, curved metal, the man gave it a ferocious tug.

The force of the pull, combined with the boat's lurch, threw her off her feet. She hit the rain-dampened hull and screamed as the hook trapped her hand against the canoe's bow, crushing her fingers.

Sam's vision blurred as pain overrode her senses. Her fingers felt as though they'd been set on fire. She tried to get her spare hand behind the hook to pull it off, but her stalker gave an extra-sharp tug, increasing the pressure, and Sam cried out again.

The man stood on the edge of the dock, legs braced on the wood, both hands wrapped around the rope as he pulled her closer in long, easy drags. She couldn't look away. The wolfish, blood-hungry smile dominated his face, as his terrible gray eyes laughed at her while the rain drenched him. She would be at the edge of the dock in a few seconds. *What then? Will he use the ax or one of the knives? Will he take my finger before or after he kills me?*

She had no energy left to fight him or even to free her burning, trapped hand. Her eyes dropped and widened as movement underneath the dock caught her attention. Bodies were pulling themselves out of the weedy area below the pier, dripping water as they clung to the dark supports. *There's so many of them. Are they all his?*

Gaunt, sightless, decaying faces turned upward, toward the dock, and sallow hands rose to dig their nails into the wood, applying their weight to the decaying structure. Even in the canoe, Sam could hear the scratching, scraping noises they produced. The man heard them, too, and his smile faltered as he glanced toward his feet. He was just in time to see the wood splinter below his boots, then the dock gave out, and he plunged through the hole and into the waiting arms of his victims.

CHAPTER 18

THE PRESSURE ON THE hook slackened, then the canoe bumped into the edge of the dock and rebounded. Sam was finally able to force her left hand under the hook. She pulled as hard as she could, digging it out of the wood until she was able to free her right hand. Then she slumped back, clutching her injured fingers to her chest as she watched the water below the dock froth while the gray-eyed man fought for his life.

She finally let herself rest as the exhaustion from the stress and sleepless night crashed over her. Rain dripped from her drenched hair and ran down her face as she leaned against the boat's side. She focused on breathing, drawing ragged breaths into her aching lungs, until the frantic, churning of the water subsided.

The waves spent themselves on the shore, and at last, the lake was still again, save for the multitude of tiny ripples created by the rain. Sam shivered. She couldn't see any sign of the man or the bodies that had claimed him. Except for the hole in the dock and her aching fingers, it was almost as though the last half hour had never happened. Sam let her eyes close.

She didn't know how long she stayed there, shivering and nursing her throbbing hand, but the rain had eased to a drizzle when something nudged the canoe. Sam jolted to alertness and grabbed at the boat's side, afraid she might be thrown out, but the motion was gentle. The canoe slid across the water, toward the shore, until its base ground to a halt in the dirt. Sam craned her neck to look over both sides of the boat but couldn't see anything in the murky water.

She was freezing; the rain had sapped all of the warmth from her body. She pushed herself to her feet and stumbled out of the boat, willing her shaking legs to take her weight.

The surrounding forest seemed alive in a way she'd never seen it before, as though the rain had woken a multitude of hibernating beasts. Birds chattered among themselves, and farther up the mountain a wild animal called out. Sam stood on the shore for a moment, uncertain about what she should do and where she should go.

"Sam." The voice was raspy and faint, as though its owner was speaking through a damaged larynx. Sam turned and saw the corpse, her companion for the last three days, standing half a dozen paces behind her. The hollows where his eyes belonged watched her carefully, and he seemed to have posed himself to look as unthreatening as possible.

Sam let her eyes rove over him, taking in the tattered hiking clothes, the shoulder-length bronze hair, and the skin that she thought must have been pale even before his death. She took a half step toward him. "Ian? Ian McCarthy?"

The cadaver's cracked lips twitched into a smile, and he gave a small nod, then held his closed fist toward her. "We found these in his pocket."

Sam held out her hand, and Ian dropped the ranger's car keys into it. His fingers, clammy and spongy, brushed her hand, but Sam found it less repulsive than she'd expected. She swallowed thickly as she stared at the keys. "Thank you. For saving me. For everything."

Ian turned his sightless eyes toward the car. "The ranger is still alive, but not for much longer. I treated the wound as well as I could, but…it's becoming harder to remember…who I used to be…what I used to know…" He exhaled a lungful of sticky, moist air and shook his head. "You'll need to hurry, Sam."

"Okay." Sam took a step backward but couldn't bring herself to turn away. "I'll make sure your…your body is found. And the others. You'll have a proper burial."

Another smile fluttered across the corpse's face, peeling up the edges of the decayed skin on his cheeks. "You know, all of that becomes surprisingly unimportant when you're dead. But I would be grateful if my family knew what happened."

"Of course. I'll make sure."

"And you're welcome to use the paintings. They're as much yours as they are mine."

Her drained mind couldn't understand what he meant, but she nodded anyway.

The corpse gave her a final, gentle smile. "Goodbye, Sam."

The rain had settled to infrequent spits, but it was still enough to make Sam shiver as Ian turned and started toward the lake. She stared at the car keys in her hand, blinking back tears, then drew a shuddering breath as Ian's words filtered through to her. *Brandon's still alive.*

She ran to the car. Brandon had been moved to the passenger seat and leaned against the door. Ian had cut off Brandon's shirt and turned it into bandages, which had been wrapped around his torso. Sam held a shaking hand in front of his open mouth and felt his breath—weak but enduring—on her fingertips. She slid into the driver's seat, buckled the belt, and put the keys into the ignition. As the car's motor roared to life, she glanced back at the lake.

Sunlight had broken through the rain clouds and painted large golden streaks across the water's surface. The cabin, beautiful and rustic, was as much a part of the lake as the rocks. It watched over its surroundings. Ian knelt on the dock's edge, in his familiar crouched pose. He turned toward Sam and raised a hand in farewell. Sam returned the gesture, and the corpse slid forward, over the edge of the dock, to plunge into the water.

CHAPTER 19

WHEN ARRANGED IN ORDER, the paintings had a startling impact. They started with brief glimpses of the man moving like a wraith through the trees, then focused on his face and his harsh gray eyes. From there, the paintings moved on to show his victims fighting for their lives, and ultimately losing. The finger was cut off. Then the bodies were thrown off the dock, plunging below the lake's surface, where they would become tangled in weeds and consumed by fish and insects. The narrative was brutal and shocking, but it also held something of a distorted elegance: man pitted against man in nature's arena.

Sam stood with her back to a pillar near the center of the spacious, well-lit room, her right hand discreetly held behind her back so that the splint wouldn't be too obvious. The gray-eyed man's grappling hook had broken two of her fingers. Looking at the paintings, though, Sam could only feel grateful for how lightly she'd escaped.

The Heritage's patrons walked through the display, murmuring to one another. Occasionally, one would approach her, shake her hand, and congratulate her on the exhibition. They used words such as *impactful* and *mesmerizing*, and she received at least three requests for her business card from other gallery owners and art critics.

Brandon inclined his head toward her and murmured into her ear, "They love it."

Sam could only manage a weak, choked chuckle. It still felt unreal to her; in the eight days following her escape from the lake, she'd spent half of her time in the hospital and the other half assisting the police in their investigation. Even though the paintings had been returned to her a few days after she'd arrived home, she'd barely had a chance to look at them, let alone think about them.

She hadn't made the decision to exhibit the paintings lightly. They depicted real events, from memories of a real life that had been lost. But Ian McCarthy's blessing had been the deciding factor. *"You're welcome to use the paintings. They're as much yours as they are mine."*

Brandon casually bumped the back of his right hand into her left, and Sam felt a smile grow over her face as their fingers entwined.

Following their escape, she'd visited the ranger in hospital and celebrated the small triumphs with him as he was moved from ICU to the general ward then finally discharged. Following that, they'd worked together to help the police find the gray-eyed man's cabin. Sam only had a vague idea of where it had been, but Brandon was familiar with the mountain's landscape, and together, they'd been able to pin down the approximate location.

She'd found herself gravitating toward the ranger and his unassuming, steady kindness. His shy invitation for a date couldn't have come soon enough.

Sam was slowly learning to trust him in a way she hadn't trusted anyone since her mother's passing. When she'd told him about the cadaver who had guided her dreams and saved both of their lives, he hadn't scoffed or laughed like she'd been afraid he would, but accepted it with a quiet "wow."

She'd been much more selective about what she'd shared with the police. Instead of telling them the gray-eyed man had been dragged into the lake, she said he'd fallen through the rotten wood. Everyone seemed content with that explanation; when his corpse was fished out of the lake, he'd had lacerations across his body and a substantial head wound. The coroner's report said he'd hit his head while falling through the hole and drowned.

It had taken some time to discover his name. In the end, Uncle Earnest's guess had been half-right: although he was very much a human, the man was Michael Paluhik. He belonged to the trio of hikers to first disappear around the lake, and his body had, obviously, never been recovered.

Friends had described Michael as quiet and shy, but his diary, a tattered book found on one of his cabin's shelves, painted a very different picture. He'd grown up with impulses that he hadn't understood and had struggled to contain. His diary talked about wanting to kill his mother, his siblings, and even his friends. The entries went into increasingly graphic detail about the ways he would do it, the expressions he could picture on their faces, and how he imagined their blood would taste.

He'd managed to control his urges until that fateful backpacking trip with his two closest friends. In the privacy of the woods, he'd murdered them both with his camping knife and dragged their bodies off the path so the deaths would seem accidental when they were found. He'd taken a single memento from each body: their index fingers.

Knowing that his crimes would be uncovered if he returned to civilization, Michael built himself a life inside the forest. He knew enough about wilderness survival to live off the land and find clean water, and he occasionally took the two-day hike to the nearest town to purchase anything he wasn't able to build for himself.

According to his diary, the impulses had grown stronger with each passing year. At first, he'd only taken one or two lives a year, choosing from among the hikers he'd watched on Trail T-1, which ran near his cabin and he considered his domain. But eventually, the cravings had grown so severe that he'd started killing every few months.

Sam would have been his nineteenth victim in eight years.

She still couldn't understand how or why Ian and his companions had retained their autonomy after death. She and Brandon had bandied theories back and forth; Brandon had found an outdated web page that talked about Harob Lake being home to otherworldly spirits and thought that some sort of energy had sustained the victims' awareness. Sam thought Ian, the last hiker to go missing, might have had some sort of spiritual aptitude, and his death had been the catalyst for its unleashing and had, in turn, woken the other bodies.

Either way, they owed Ian their lives. His funeral was scheduled for the following morning. Because they'd worked so closely with the police to retrieve his body, both Sam and Brandon had received an invitation to attend.

Even though the dead man didn't have a high opinion of funerals, Sam was looking forward to seeing him finally laid to rest. She'd ordered a special bunch of liriope flowers, which had grown in abundance in the lake he had become so fond of.

Sam leaned her head against Brandon's shoulder and felt her smile widen as he rubbed her hand in response.

WHOSE
WOODS
THESE ARE

MORROW WOODS, AN ANCIENT tangle of conifers at the edge of a rural town, sprawled in front of Anna, and she slowed her car to get a better look. She hadn't seen the forest in over a decade, but amazingly, it was almost exactly how she remembered it.

A few things had changed, though. She'd tried to find the parking lot where her family had always left their car when they'd come there to camp, and she was surprised to discover it no longer existed. A gate blocked her access to a weedy field that had once been a dirt patch studded with markers.

Anna glanced from the cordoned-off parking lot to the mass of trees behind it and shrugged her seat belt a little higher on her shoulder. She turned her car back onto the gravel road that ran along the edge of the woods and followed it for a few minutes. When she found a shrubby stretch of grass, she eased her car off the road and carefully parked it where it was hidden behind a thick clump of bushes.

The trees loomed above her as she stepped out of the car. She inhaled deeply, savoring the light scent of the pines and organic decay, and listened for familiar birdcalls. The air was a far cry from the lazy smog of the city, and it pulled her back to childhood memories of hiking through the trees and struggling to set up tents on uneven ground. Anna grinned at the forest, feeling as if she were greeting an old friend.

Something else was new about the woods: a chain-link fence, nearly two meters high, stood between her and the trees. It ran as far as she could see in both directions.

Anna couldn't remember seeing a fenced-off wood before, and it made her pause. She wondered why a small, quiet town like Gillespie—which she'd left just a few kilometers behind her, hidden by the rolling hills and scrappy patches of trees—would spend what must have been a small fortune on segregating itself from nature. Perhaps the forest had become a restricted area or they were trying to keep people, like her, from damaging it.

Or are they trying to stop something from getting out? The area was too far south for wolves, and there weren't any bears in that part of the country. *What else, then? Wild boars? Exceptionally annoying squirrels?*

Anna snorted with laughter and pulled her backpack out of the car's trunk. She couldn't imagine a single creature in the region that needed a fence to keep it contained, which meant the forest must have been turned into a protected area. She felt slightly guilty about her plans to trespass, but a childhood full of camping had taught her how to respect nature. She knew she could leave the woods as clean and healthy as it was before she'd entered it.

Besides, she needed this. The hike was like a closure somehow—a final goodbye to her father, the nature lover, who had brought his family to the woods every year until Anna had turned fourteen. The catharsis was too important for her to turn back just because of a fence.

Scaling the chain-link barricade turned out to be harder than she'd expected, though. The fence was only a little taller than she was, but it took a good bit of heaving to throw her heavy bag over the top. It hit the ground on the other side with a hard *thump*, and Anna cringed, hoping none of the equipment had been broken.

She hooked her fingers through the holes in the chain-link and climbed it with less speed and much less grace than she'd hoped for. Still, she made it over the sharp wires at the top without cutting herself. She dropped to the ground on the other side, dusted the dirt off her cargo pants, heaved the backpack over her shoulders, and began walking.

As she moved deeper into the trees, the gentle downward slope gave way to a pine-needle-littered forest floor pocked with holes and exposed roots. Anna picked a dead branch off the ground and used it as a walking stick to prod at the piles of detritus to make sure she wasn't about to step in a concealed hole and break her ankle.

The air around her buzzed with life; the scent of plants and organic decay was rich and heady, and the ground felt pleasantly springy under her feet. *I should move somewhere like this,* she thought absently, running a hand over a tree's bark. *The city's killing me.*

She kept her pace slow, taking the chance to enjoy her surroundings and fill her lungs with fresh oxygen. The day was warmer than the forecast had predicted, and before long, she was too sweaty to keep her jacket on.

Just over an hour into the hike, her surroundings began to change. The lush green grasses and vines started to disappear; sickly, spindly plants took their places. The pine trees seemed to grow taller, but their trunks were darker and had fewer low branches. What needles she could see were discolored and looked unhealthy. A flicker of dark amber on one of the trees caught her attention. She stopped to look at it and found she was breathing heavily despite her slow pace.

She had to step right up to the tree before she recognized the amber color as sap. Dribbles of long-dried golden juice hung like stalactites from a six-inch gash in the bark. Anna ran her fingers over the cool, smooth substance. *What sort of jerk hacks into a live tree like this?*

She turned back to her path, but her steps faltered as she began to notice cuts in other trees. Some were only little nicks, but others were deep slashes that cut into the center of the trunk. A few of the trees had been damaged so badly that they had died. Held in place by lifeless roots, they stood waiting for rot or a strong storm to bring them down.

She'd never seen damage like that when she'd camped there before. *It must be why the city put the fence up. Makes sense.* She guessed clueless campers, bored teenagers, or possibly even someone with anger management problems had come in and cut up the trees, so they were protecting the forest until it could regenerate.

But as she moved farther through the forest, she had to wonder how much good the fence was doing. Some of the cuts looked fresh, as if they'd been made within the last month. *Why, though? What's the point of walking into the heart of a wood to spend hours cutting at trees?*

She stopped beside a tree with four deep slashes at her head height. They looked only a few days old. She stared at the honey-gold dribbles, suddenly feeling much less confident about spending the night alone in the woods. *What if whoever did this comes back?*

Anna turned to look at the path she'd come from. It wasn't too late to turn back, but that would mean wasting an entire day, not to mention the equipment she'd bought and the gas she'd burned driving there…

"Jeez," she muttered, and the heavy air around her seemed to swallow her voice. She'd come to the woods to remember her father on the anniversary of his death. She *could* leave, but she knew she would hate herself if she did.

The forest was vast, too, and her intended camping site was still a long way off. The chances of two strangers bumping into each other in the maze of trees had to be tiny. *Besides, I'm not completely defenseless. I brought a knife.*

Comforted, Anna turned back to her path. She picked up her pace, stepping briskly, only pausing every twenty minutes to check her compass.

She reached her destination, the river, late in the afternoon. The trees growing alongside it were healthier and less damaged, though they still grew taller than those at the entrance to the woods had. Anna sat on the rocky bank of the river for a few minutes, admiring how clear the liquid was as it rushed over the smooth pebbles. She caught flashes of motion in some of the more stagnant areas and was pleased to see that, no matter what had happened to the trees, the fish population was still thriving.

The air was filled with birdsong and animal calls. She closed her eyes and listened, trying to pick out sounds she recognized. She caught the high, light trills of tree creepers and thought she heard a hawk's screech in the distance. Other calls she couldn't identify, though: some cackling, some trilling, and one especially strange noise that sounded like broken laughter coming from a long way away.

Since she'd stopped moving, she was chilling quickly as her sweat dried. The sun was sinking lower, and she knew she needed to set her tent up before it became too dark to see. The ground around the stream was uneven and sloped, so she backtracked for a few minutes until she came across a relatively flat glade. She shrugged her camping backpack off then spent a few minutes clearing rocks, leaves, and sticks away from where she planned to put her tent.

The light was already dimming toward twilight, so she moved quickly as she assembled the two-person tent. Her father had sold his camping equipment many years previously, so Anna had bought a cheap model for this trip.

She had to admit, though, as she fitted the canvas over the tent poles, camping was more enjoyable with company. She'd broken up with her boyfriend only a month before her father had passed, and she was feeling the isolation.

"Still," she muttered, forcing a metal peg into the soft ground with her hands, "it's nice not to have to argue about what we eat."

Her parents had never agreed on what food to bring. Her father would have wanted sausages, steaks, onion, and eggs, all fried over the fire. Her mother, practical and cautious, had always insisted that meat was not safe to consume after spending the day in a warm backpack and suggested sandwiches and canned food instead.

As an adult, Anna tended to side more with her mother. The last place anyone wanted to get food poisoning was in the middle of the woods. Still, they'd eaten dubious sausages and steaks for ten years' worth of camping trips without any disasters, and because her visit was a testament to her father, she'd brought a pack of sausages wrapped in a small cooling pack.

Anna finished setting up the tent in good time. The ground wasn't firm enough for the pegs to anchor it properly, so she placed some largish, clean rocks inside each corner of the tarp base. She kicked and scraped the dead pine needles away from an area in front of her tent, creating a large circle of exposed dirt. A quick search turned up several more rocks, which she built into a ring to protect and contain her fire.

She needed to have water nearby before she lit it, so Anna pulled one of the larger pots out of her backpack and walked to the stream. The sun was halfway set, and the twilight played strange tricks on her eyes, blending trees with shadows. As she neared the stream, she once again heard the strange noise that sounded like wild laughter. She stopped short. The sound was much closer than it had been before and seemed too deep to belong to a bird. *An animal, maybe?*

The sound broke off, and Anna strained to hear it again. The atmosphere seemed different somehow, and she realized that all other sounds—birds, animals, and even the insects—had quieted following the strange call, leaving only the rustling of the trees.

The skin on her arms prickled into goose bumps. Suddenly wanting a fire more than anything else, she broke into a jog.

She was relieved to finally push through a patch of bushes and find herself at the bank of the river. A thinner canopy above her allowed more of the waning sunlight through, and Anna paused to soak it up for a moment before kneeling beside the running water and dunking the pot into it. The fish were gone, probably hidden somewhere to sleep for the night.

Anna stood slowly as the strangest sensation crept over her. She felt as though she were being scrutinized, as if her every movement were being followed. Anna lived in the city, where there were eyes everywhere. At any minute, she could have half a dozen gazes on her, but she'd never before felt *watched* like she did at that moment.

You're in a forest. There's no one here.

She turned in a slow circle, pot clasped in both hands, as she scanned the woods around her. *It's so quiet. Even the trees seem to be holding their breath.*

Then the wind changed direction, and a strong, foul musk invaded her nose. Anna gagged, and water sloshed over the lip of her pot. It was unlike anything she'd smelled before; it reminded her of rotten eggs and decaying meat, with a bitter, metallic undertone.

She didn't wait any longer but began jogging up the incline toward her tent. Water spilled out of the pot and soaked her pants and hiking shoes, but she didn't slow down. By the time she reached her camp, she could no longer smell the odor, but it hung in her mind like a fly she couldn't swat away.

"No wonder they built a fence," she muttered, setting her half-full pot beside her tent and rubbing at her nose. "I would, too, if it kept me from smelling that."

Anna chuckled to herself then kicked off her wet shoes and crawled into the tent. She opened the backpack and rifled through it until she found her comfy sneakers. They were no good for hiking—she'd brought them to wear at night while she sat by the fire—but they would do well enough until her hiking shoes dried.

She climbed out of her tent and began gathering dry firewood. The sun was almost completely set, so she searched by feel more than sight. She'd badly underestimated how long setting up the tent and the fire pit would take, probably because last time she'd been camping, she'd had two parents to help.

She put a small stack of fire starters in the center of the pit then stacked dry pine needles and small sticks on top. She lit them and sat to watch as the flames licked over and eventually caught onto the wood. Once the kindling had caught, she put a few larger pieces of wood on top and began pulling food and the frying pan out of her backpack.

The day's walk had drained her, and she almost settled on eating canned fruit for dinner, but she knew her father would have been disappointed. *"If you're going camping, you'd better do it properly,"* he'd once said while he poked at the sizzling sausages and her mother dourly buttered bread.

"This is for you, Dad," Anna said, putting two of the sausages in the pan and setting it over the growing flames. She'd never felt so lonely.

The air chilled rapidly as night overtook the woods, and Anna pulled on her spare jackets. Twice, she thought she caught traces of the rotting smell on the wind, but it passed quickly. *Maybe something died down by the river.*

She kept the fire small, just hot enough to cook the sausages and warm her a little. She sat on the ground close to its heat as shadows danced around the edge of the clearing. The daytime birds had fallen silent shortly after sunset, and owls and night animals had taken over. Their hollow calls floated to her through the night air.

She pulled the sausages off the fire and ate them straight out of the pan, savoring the warmth as it pooled in her stomach and spread outward. They were overcooked—better over than under, her mother would have said—but because she was famished, they tasted like a feast.

She'd also packed dessert: an apple with its core cut out and a chocolate bar pushed into the hole. She rolled the apple, which was wrapped in foil, into the coals to heat through. It was another of her father's favorites, and one dish her mother had approved of.

While she waited for it to cook, she went back to her tent to inflate her blow-up mattress and unroll her sleeping bag. The fire's light was strong enough to come through the tent's canvas and illuminate her. It threw jumping shadows on the wall opposite. They seemed to move independently of each other, some traveling left while others went right, and she paused her work to watch them.

Then she realized the light was growing dimmer. *The fire shouldn't need more wood yet.* She'd put two branches on it only a few minutes previously—but as she turned around to look at it, the campfire went out with a harsh sizzle, plunging the tent into darkness.

Anna's heart leaped into her throat as she stayed still, listening. The woods outside were perfectly silent. Then she smelled the stench again—thick, cloistering, and nauseating. She had to suppress the urge to spit it out of her mouth.

Fear spiked through her, and she scrambled for the flashlight in her backpack. The pine trees were too thick to let any more than a few scraps of moonlight through, leaving her nearly blind, and she struggled to find the flashlight among the spare clothes, blankets, maps, and cutlery.

She finally found it in a side pocket and turned it on with shaking hands, holding it like a sword in front of her body as she advanced out of the tent. The air felt colder than it had before, as though the temperature had dropped five degrees in the two minutes she'd been inside. Her breath misted in front of her face, and her nose started to burn from drawing in the chilled air.

She stopped just outside the tent and roved her flashlight in a semicircle, searching for movement. Tree branches twitched and shook in the wind. Her flashlight's beam was too narrow to light much; all it could do was tease her with small snapshots of her surroundings.

She moved toward the fire. It was completely dead; there weren't even any coals left. Anna pressed a shaking finger to one of the logs. It was still warm, but not hot, and felt slightly damp. Unnerved, she pulled away from the dead fire and swung her light across the border of the glade again. *What could make the coals wet?*

The answer came to her quickly. *The pot of water, of course. Did someone find me and tip it over the fire?*

She turned to where she'd left the pot beside the tent. Chills crawled up her spine as she dipped a finger over the rim and found it was still filled with water. *Then what...?*

The sickly, thick smell still permeated the air, though it seemed to be lessening. Anna rotated slowly, trying to hold the light steady as she searched the trees. She knew she had only two options: pack up and hike out of the woods as quickly as possible or stay the night.

It wasn't much of a choice. The hike alone was five hours, never mind the time it would take to pack her equipment, and she would be much, much slower in the pitch black. By the time she left the woods, it would be dawn—or close to it—and she wasn't sure she had the energy to stay alert and conscious of her surroundings until then.

Looks like we'll be spending the night here.

Anna shivered and retreated into her tent, zipping it closed behind herself. She pulled her knife out of her bag and sat for a long time, too scared to sleep, gripping the flashlight in one hand and the knife in the other. Eventually, exhaustion dampened the anxiety enough to let her crawl into the sleeping bag and close her eyes, but she kept a firm grip on the knife just in case.

Her last thoughts were about the smell, which was almost gone, and the calls of an owl perched somewhere above her tent.

She dreamed about the last time her father had brought them camping to Morrow Woods, when she'd been fourteen years old. They'd stopped at the town that bordered the forest to pick up a few last-minute supplies. Her father had gone to see if he could find a more up-to-date map of the woods, while she and her mother bought fresh bread, a small square of butter, and a tub of live bait for fishing in the river.

Her father was gone for a long time, and when he came back, he looked older somehow. He'd pulled Anna's mother off to one side and talked to her in a hurried, hushed tone. When he turned back to Anna, he put on one of the most forced smiles she'd ever seen.

"Your mother and I were thinking, Annie," he said. "There's

another forest an hour's drive away that we've been wanting to visit. We thought we'd give it a try."

"What? Now?" Anna glanced out the shop's window. She could see the edge of the woods not even fifteen minutes' walk away. "But we always camp here!"

Her father just laughed and ushered her back into the car then drove them to the smaller, tamer pine forest he'd mentioned. It had been nowhere near as pretty as Morrow Woods was, and Anna hadn't been able to understand why he'd wanted to visit it so badly all of a sudden.

Anna woke up with a start. It was still dark. The flashlight illuminated the inside of the tent, turning it into a small, golden cave. The smell was back, saturating the air. She held still, wrapped in her sleeping bag, knife clasped in one hand and flashlight in the other, listening hard. She thought she could hear breathing, but it was so well disguised by the rustling trees that she couldn't be sure.

Then the sound from the day before split the silence. A twisted, broken, wailing laugh came from just outside the tent's entrance.

Anna bit the inside of her cheek to keep herself from crying out as the laugh cut off abruptly and silence rushed in to fill the void.

Don't move, she thought as she tried to control her heavy breathing. *Don't let it hear you.*

The silence stretched out. An itch crawled across Anna's back, but she didn't dare move to scratch it. Sweat was drenching her clothes and beading on her forehead despite the cold, and she struggled to slow her thundering heart.

Szzzzzzzzrch…

Anna jumped at the new noise but couldn't immediately tell where it was coming from. The source became horribly clear when she saw the zip at the tent's entrance was moving along its track, pulled by a force outside the tent, creating a gaping hole in her meager fort.

The time for silence was over. Anna scrambled out of her sleeping bag, kicking at the thick, fluffy fabric when it got stuck over her feet, then scrambled backward until she was pressed against the rear of the tent.

Her sudden movement didn't disturb the zipper's progress. It glided in a smooth arc, and as the released part of the door began to flop out of the way, she caught a glimpse of the outside.

She focused her flashlight on it, hoping to blind the intruder or at least see it, but whatever was unzipping her tent stayed out of view. She could see the trees, twitching and shivering, and even parts of her ruined fire, where the foil-wrapped, half-baked apple still sat in the blackened patch, winking at her like silver treasure.

Szzzzzzzzzrch…tch!

The zipper hit the end of its runner, leaving the door wide open. Anna's hands were shaking too badly to hold the flashlight steady; it jittered over the opening but failed to show her the opener.

133

"Who's there?" Anna called. She had never heard a silence as complete as what followed her voice.

The trees had fallen still. The animals of the night seemed to hold their breaths. She heard no sound at all, not even the gentle tap of falling pine needles.

The smell invaded her nose with each breath, turning her stomach and making her dizzy. She pressed herself against the back of the tent as she waited, her shaking hands pointing the flashlight and knife toward the tent's opening.

Then claws, large and viciously sharp, plunged through the canvas at her back. One snagged her jacket, and she lurched free with a shriek.

Carrying only the flashlight and knife, Anna threw herself through the doorway and into the dark embrace of the night. At once, noise returned to the woods, swelling and growing in pitch as though the trees were exhausted from holding their breath. Birds—both those that belonged to the day and those that lived in the night—began to cry. Animals screamed. The wind, after holding still for so long, burst through the trees and brought down a shower of pine needles. The sound surrounded her, deafening her. She could barely hear her own gasping as she ran for the cover of the trees.

Something large, dark, and fast was racing around the edge of the tent. It was moving too quickly for her eyes to fix on it, and she only got a vague impression of ragged clothing and brightly white teeth. As it ran, it called to her, adding its hideous laughter to the noise of the woods.

It—whatever it was, human, animal, or something else entirely—darted across her path. Anna was running too quickly to change direction or stop, so she raised the point of her knife and let her momentum force it into the creature's chest.

Blood sprayed from where the blade pierced its flesh. The creature wailed, and its scream was a terrible cacophony that filled Anna's head and made her ears feel as if they were about to explode. She closed her eyes, let go of the knife, and continued running, her blood-dampened right hand held in front of her face to shield her from branches, her left hand doing a poor job of focusing the flashlight on her path. Her breath sticky and thick in her lungs, she ran until the woods quieted and the stench left her nose. She ran until her legs ached and her arms throbbed from scratches. She ran until she thought her heart was about to burst and her lungs burned.

Then she let herself fall to the ground. She was too exhausted, physically and emotionally, to cry, so she lay on the floor of pine needles and roots, doing her best to draw breath quickly enough to replenish her oxygen-depleted muscles. She could hear the gentle rustle of the trees and the occasional animal noise, but she didn't think she had been chased. The smell was gone, too.

Anna pulled herself to a sitting position and found she was dizzy. Her head throbbed, her arms stung, and her legs ached. The moon wasn't strong enough to penetrate the unnaturally tall trees, so she picked up the flashlight from where she'd dropped it and gingerly inspected her stinging forearms. They bore dozens of tiny cuts from the branches and vines she'd raced through.

She could feel some tender patches on her cheeks, too. Her right hand—the one she had held the knife in—had a pale pink, jelly-like liquid sprayed over the fingers and wrist. She tried to shake it off, but it clung to her skin. Disgusted, she picked up a handful of pine needles and used them to rub off most of the liquid. Then she brushed the hand over her sweater and jeans to clean it further.

She had no idea which direction she'd run in or how far she was from the fence. She knew she could find her direction reasonably well once the sun came up, but until then, she couldn't risk moving farther into the woods, so she huddled at the base of the tree.

Anna didn't let herself fall asleep as she waited. Every ten minutes, she got up and paced in circles to ward off the exhaustion that threatened to lower her guard. She focused on searching for the smell, assuming that, as long as the air was sweet, danger wasn't too close.

The night air was freezing, and before long, she was shivering. Her jacket did a reasonable job of protecting her top half, but the jeans she'd slept in did nothing to warm her.

She was immeasurably relieved when dawn arrived. Anna felt exhausted and fragile, as if she were held together with fine threads that might break at any moment. The trees were too thick for her to see the sun directly, but she clambered to her feet and guessed which direction the light was coming from. She then turned herself in a quarter circle, so she would be walking south. She knew the park was north of the town, so if she walked far enough, she would eventually arrive at the fence.

With the light at her back and the flashlight batteries starting to fail, she began walking as briskly as her sore legs would let her. After about an hour, she stumbled on the river that wound through the woods. She was parched, so she stopped for a drink and to wash the scratches on her arms. Then she followed the river for another kilometer before she recognized the section she'd visited the night before.

She was tempted to bypass her camp entirely, but curiosity and necessity won out. Her camping equipment had been expensive. Besides, she didn't fancy the idea of walking for five hours without water or food. Anna traced the path from the river to the clearing where she'd set up camp, and stopped at the edge of the trees.

Her campsite was wrecked. The tent was shredded. Its torn tarp, still tethered to the ground with pegs and rocks, flapped limply in the breeze. Her gear had been ripped from the bag and lay about the clearing like shrapnel. Even the stones she'd used to make the fireplace had been hurled away from the cold charcoal and half-burned branches. The trees surrounding the clearing had suffered, too. Deep gashes marred their trunks, and many of the lower branches had been torn off.

Anna stumbled through the remains, stunned, hardly absorbing the sights. She paused to pick up one of her saucepans—one side had been crushed in, and it was pocked with holes. She dropped it to the ground.

What did this? What's strong enough to cause this much damage?

She didn't stay long; it felt too unsafe to linger, and she saw almost nothing worth salvaging. Her backpack had been torn in half, but she managed to tie one of the pieces up well enough to act as a bag. Into it, she loaded the only undamaged saucepan, a spare jacket, tent pegs, and an empty water bottle. She also found her shoes—thankfully intact, though a little dirty—and switched them with the comfy sneakers she'd been wearing. Everything else had been destroyed.

Anna paused to look around the scene one final time before turning back toward the river. She had a long hike from her campsite to the edge of the woods, and she knew she would be grateful for a full water bottle.

She'd been drained by the fear, the running, and the night without sleep, and Anna found herself stumbling over the exposed roots and rocks as she made her way down the incline. She kept her eyes focused on her feet and didn't look up until she was nearly at the water's edge.

A girl was standing in her way. Anna stopped short, nearly crying out from shock. The girl faced away from her, watching the water swirl over the smooth river stones. She was wearing a dark, tattered dress, and her thick black hair was matted with twigs and small leaves.

Anna gaped at her, trying to understand what she was seeing. *What's a child doing in these woods? Does she live here?*

As the girl swayed gently from side to side, a new thought entered Anna's mind. *Does she know what attacked me last night?*

At that moment, the wind changed, and Anna gagged on the sudden thick stench that blew over her. It was much stronger than it had been the night before. An automatic fear response made Anna stumble backward, her shoes slipping on the forest floor, until her back hit a tree.

The girl turned languidly, and Anna clamped a hand over her mouth to stop herself from screaming. The child's eyes were entirely black: no iris, no whites, just black gashes sitting in the impossibly pale face.

No…they're not eyes…they're holes.

Where her hands should have been were claws. Thick and curved, they were as long as Anna's forearm. They draped down the side of the child's dress and nearly touched the ground. Something was also protruding from her chest. Something metallic and familiar. *My knife.*

The girl opened her mouth and laughed. Her eyes—or where her eyes should have been—crinkled, and her red lips spread wide. The harsh, cruel sound that came out of her throat was far louder than any human could have made.

Anna dropped the water bottle and started running. The smell was making her dizzy, so she held her breath as long as she could. Her aching legs screamed under this new strain, but she didn't let herself stop as the laughter followed her up the incline.

She ran through the demolished camp, not even sparing a glance at the slashed trees or shredded tent. She thought the creature was right on her heels, just waiting for her to slow down before it dug its claws into her back.

She was exhausted. As the smell and the laughter gradually faded, Anna let her sprint slow to a brisk walk. Her limbs were shaking badly, but she didn't stop moving. She knew which direction she needed to go to get out of the infernal forest, and she focused on walking as quickly as her burning muscles would move.

She hadn't collected any water, and by midday, she was parched, but the reappearance of healthier trees and vines encouraged her to keep walking. The cuts in the trunks soon disappeared, and she thought the atmosphere felt lighter.

Then she unexpectedly broke through the trees and found herself facing the fence. Its new significance hit her as she gazed up at it with mingled relief and revulsion. *What's the chance it has nothing to do with protecting the woods, and everything to do with protecting the town?*

She didn't want to linger inside the forest for even a moment more than she had to, so she threw her makeshift bag over the fence then wrapped her fingers through the metal wires and began to climb. The effort drained her remaining energy, and when her feet touched down on the other side, she sank to the grass and closed her eyes. The sun, something she hadn't felt since she'd entered the woods, played over her skin. She smiled, then her smile turned into tears. She covered her face with her sweaty, dirty hands as the enormity of the events finally caught up to her.

She didn't have long to rest, though. As she took a deep breath to clear her pounding head, she caught traces of the bitter, rotten scent she'd come to associate with danger.

She sat up, her fear returning and feeding energy into her aching joints and weary bones. She scanned the edge of the woods but couldn't see anything. Still, she stood, feeling the blisters in her feet burn, and began walking again. She made a guess about which direction she'd left her car, and after forty minutes, she found it, still hidden behind the bushes. She slid into the driver's seat with a sigh of immense gratitude.

Anna was famished and thirsty, so she stopped by the town's small eatery. She must have looked ghastly—the patrons all stared at her with either curiosity or pity as she pulled herself onto the stool in front of the counter.

The waitress, young and plump, with a short crop of black hair, eyed her cautiously. "You okay?"

"Yeah," Anna said, rubbing at her raw eyes. She'd decided on a white lie during the drive into town. "Been backpacking. Couldn't find a hotel for last night. Can I get the biggest breakfast you sell and a jug of water?"

"Oh, yeah." The girl's demeanor changed instantly as she motioned at the line cook. "Backpacking can sure do a number on you, eh? I went through England last year, and I stayed in a place with roaches everywhere and cold showers. I thought I was going to die."

Anna laughed weakly, but her attention was focused on the progress of her breakfast on the grill.

An aged, grizzled man sitting next to her chuckled. "If I didn't know better, I would've thought you'd come out of the woods."

"Lay off it, Bern," the waitress said, scorn and affection mingling in her voice. "She don't want to listen to your horror stories, I'm sure."

Anna waited until the waitress had gone to clear off one of the tables, then she turned to Bern. "What about the woods?"

The man's cracked lips split into a grin, and she saw that he was missing at least half of his teeth. "Oh, you haven't heard of the monster, huh? It's our local legend. I'm the resident expert on it, you know."

Anna leaned on the bench, indicating that she was giving him her full attention, and he continued gladly.

"Twenty years ago, those woods used to be very popular for camping. Lovely place, it was, with lots of wildlife and a big stream weaving through it. Then, all of a sudden, campers started disappearing. At first, the police thought it was particularly bad luck that three couples had gotten lost on the same weekend, but then they found the bodies. It was a real horror show. They were torn apart—hardly recognizable—with their organs scattered about them like a halo.

"Then the search parties—the ones who had been looking for the missing people—started coming forward with strange stories. Talking about seeing a little girl, and saying there was a really bad smell too. I never went into the woods, but one gent who stopped by my shop told me it gave him such bad heebie-jeebies, he'd had nightmares for a week.

"Well, the police assumed it was some sort of serial killer and called in reinforcements from nearby towns. There was a big investigation about it. Just about everyone within a ten-kilometer radius got questioned. Then some of the officers who'd been searching the woods started going missing, too. Those that got out repeated the same story—they'd been attacked by a girl with dead eyes and claws instead of hands. The cost and body count escalated. The deaths only ever happened in the woods, so eventually, the town decided the smartest thing to do was make the whole forest off-limits and put up a fence. It's been eight years since then, and whatever lives in those woods never comes out, but no one who goes in there to stay overnight is ever heard from again.

"There are a lot of stories about what the monster is and where it came from, but it usually involves witchcraft. People reckon it's either a girl who's been cursed or a witch whose spell backfired. They say it appears as a child wearing a black dress during the day, but after midnight, it transforms into an unspeakable monster and tears apart anyone it finds in its woods."

Bern finished his story and slurped at his coffee with a satisfied smile. Anna's plate of food had been placed in front of her, but she hadn't even noticed. After a moment of silence, she picked up the fork and began eating mechanically, hardly tasting the greasy food.

Anna returned to her car, unlocked the driver's door, and slid into the seat. She set it into gear and began cruising out of town, her slow speed disguising how badly she wanted to escape from its grip and never see it again.

Bern's story sounded fantastical—impossible even—except

that she had seen both the girl and the beast with her own eyes. She'd heard the laughter, smelled the overpowering odor, and looked into its ghost-white face. Bern had said no one escaped from the monster's clutches if they stayed overnight. *I got lucky. I had a weapon and used it at the right time.*

As she turned out of the town and onto the freeway, a strange smell filled the car. Anna froze, taking her foot off the accelerator and letting the car slow to a crawl before she dared raise her eyes to the rearview mirror.

The girl sat in the middle of the back seat, clawed hands draped in her lap, her wild hair framing her ghost-white face and empty eyeholes. Her mouth spread into a brilliant smile at the cleverness of her trap. Anna's eyes met the place where the girl's should have been, and the girl broke into her terrible, consuming laughter as she lunged forward.

AUTHOR'S NOTE

Forests feature heavily in my stories—and with good reason. They're alluring and dangerous all at once. They don't carry any ill will toward their visitors, but they will kill you nonetheless. I maintain that it is impossible to spend a mediocre day in the woods: it will be either a great experience…or one of the worst of your life.

Whose Woods These Are is a mix of my love of forests, my love of monster horror, and my love of ominous warnings that are ignored until too late. Sometimes I ask myself whether I would be bold enough to ignore the same cautionary red flags that my characters see. I have a stunningly powerful sense of self-preservation, but life can become dull if we don't occasionally take risks, can't it?

MANNEQUIN

I FOLLOWED GEOFF DOWN the stairs to the basement, keeping a few feet behind him as he wheezed and grunted his way to the landing. I suspected he didn't get down to the lowest level of his home very often. By the time he unlocked the heavy wooden door, his face was flushed and sweaty.

"This is it," he announced, ushering me into the concrete room. "It's a bit messy, but…"

I looked around. A single mattress, old and frayed, rested in the middle of the floor. It was surrounded by dozens of boxes of all shapes and sizes, as well as furniture shrouded in blankets. A barred, grimy window was positioned nearly at the top of the wall, letting in a narrow square of sunlight.

"Nah, it'll be fine," I said. "Fifty bucks a week, right?"

"That's right." Geoff hitched his pants as high as they would go under his bulging stomach. "You can use the bathroom and kitchen upstairs too. Just clean up after yourself and replace any groceries you take."

I nodded and approached the mattress. There were more than a few disconcerting stains on it, but Geoff had been considerate enough to leave a stack of clean sheets, blankets, and a new pillow at the bed's foot. I dropped my backpack—which held the entirety of my worldly possessions—beside the bed.

"You can move the boxes and stuff around to give yourself more room," Geoff said, hitching his pants up again as he backed toward the door. "Most of it's junk anyway. I never got around to cleaning it out. But there're some tables and a chair and stuff you can use. Just don't break anything, and we're good, okay?"

"Sure," I said. "Thanks, man."

"Later," Geoff grunted, closing the door behind himself. His huffing and groaning echoed through the room as he pulled his large frame up the stairwell.

I turned back to the basement and gave it a closer look. There was dust everywhere, and some of the boxes looked as though they hadn't been opened in decades.

When my girlfriend and I had broken up, we'd both said some pretty rash things. In retrospect, "No, don't bother. Keep the flat—I'm leaving," was one of my less-thought-out statements. I was between jobs and didn't have much in the way of savings, so it was pure good fortune that a friend at university had told me how his uncle Geoff wanted to rent out his basement. It wasn't pretty, but it was cheap and didn't come with a contract, so I couldn't complain much.

I made the bed quickly, out of eagerness to cover up the yellowed stains more than anything, then started working on making my new home more livable. There was hardly any room to stand, so I began pulling boxes away from the bed and stacked them against the walls as high as I could reach. Moving them caused showers of dust and grime to rain down on me, sending me into sneezing fits. One of the boxes rustled suspiciously. Whether it held mice or a cockroach nest, I couldn't have been sure, but I shoved it out of the way as quickly as I could and then dusted my filthy hands on my pants.

I pulled the drapery off the furniture to see if any of it was useful. I found a spindly wooden rocking chair, which I set under the narrow window, and a small, round coffee table that could double as a bedside stand and a place to eat dinner. I was tempted to make use of the giant mahogany wardrobe that was missing one door, but my clothing storage needs were better met by the coatrack I found and placed beside the door.

Most of the other furniture—the broken washing machine, the unplugged mini-fridge, the bookcase, and the foldable camping chairs—weren't much use, so I replaced their cloths and left them where they were.

One final piece of furniture, tall and narrow, was nestled in the corner, behind boxes and a few crates of what looked like children's toys. Hoping it might be useful, I struggled to it, but when I pulled away its cloth, I was disappointed and a little disturbed to find a mannequin.

The naked figure stood nearly a head taller than I did, and it was made of a smooth, slate-gray ceramic. Its masculine face was tilted upward to gaze at a corner of the room.

It seemed shockingly lifelike, even though its features were only abstract imitations of the real things. The smooth surface below its eyebrows gave the impression of a steady gaze, even though the face had no eyes. The lips were set in a hard line below high cheekbones, and its arms were held out in some unfathomable gesture. Its long fingers were devoid of nails, creases, and fingerprints, but somehow, they seemed just as human as my own.

I threw the cloth back over its bald head and rearranged the fabric to ensure every part of the mannequin was covered, then I replaced the boxes and crates in front of it.

My back was aching, and I figured the room was about as organized as I could bother making it. Dust and whorls of grime still coated the floor, and my every step kicked up small puffs. I hadn't found a broom during my cleaning, but I supposed Geoff wouldn't mind if I asked to borrow his.

I jogged up the stairs and let myself through the door at the top. Geoff's house was large, and he'd only shown me the way from the front door to the basement. As I hesitated on the landing, wondering if it would be less rude to go looking for him or to call his name, my phone beeped. I pulled it out and saw two missed messages: one from Tony, asking if I wanted to meet him and the guys at the local pub to celebrate my breakup, and another from Clive, saying they were all waiting for me.

A grin slid across my face as I texted back, saying I would be there in ten minutes. Forgetting the broom, I raced back down the stairs to get my wallet and jacket. I watched the signal on my phone as I descended, and the bars disappeared about halfway down the stairs. Clearly, the basement was a dead zone for cellular service. It was annoying, but I was willing to put up with a lot in exchange for cheap rent.

I opened the door and froze as I felt eyes watching me. I looked to my left and saw the mannequin's head, barely visible above the stacked boxes, staring in my direction.

I dropped my phone into my pocket then circled the boxes to escape the gaze of the statue. I mustn't have put the cloth on properly, I realized. A breeze from the open door had probably caused it to slide off.

A minute of puffing and clambering got me next to the mannequin. I gathered the fabric from where it was pooled around his feet then threw it back over him, being extra careful to make sure it would stay put before I extracted myself from the storage area.

The pub wasn't far from Geoff's house, and I got there in good time. My four friends were already halfway to drunk, so I made quick work of a pint of beer to catch up to them. When Clive asked me to share some of the ways my ex had wronged me, Tony had the bright idea to turn it into a drinking game.

We ordered a tray of shots and drank every time I told a story that made my friends hoot in disgust. They were predisposed to hate my ex and eager to drink, so it wasn't long before we were plastered.

We left—or we might have been kicked out; I really can't remember—shortly after midnight. I don't have any memory of finding my way home, but I did, which was a bit of a miracle, truthfully, as I'd only been there once before. I remember fumbling with my keys for what felt like an eternity before I realized I was trying to use the one from my old apartment. When I finally let myself into the house, I tried to creep toward my basement so I wouldn't wake Geoff, but I had forgotten where it was and ended up looping through the house twice before I found the right door. If Geoff heard me, he was generous enough not to disturb my drunken roving.

I woke up the next morning with a dry mouth and a splitting headache. I lay there, prone on my dust-covered mattress, for as long as I could before my bladder threatened mutiny. I pulled myself to my feet, ready to stagger upstairs, and nearly walked into the mannequin.

It stood at the foot of my bed, its arms splayed out as though to welcome an embrace, its head tilted down to angle its nonexistent gaze on me as I slept. I stumbled away from it, became tangled in my bedsheets, slipped, and caught myself on one of the boxes. My headache flared, and for a moment, I thought I would be sick on the floor. Then as I closed my eyes and breathed the dusty air through my nose, memories of the night before filtered through my mind. I remembered spinning around with the mannequin, laughing at how serious he looked and telling him he was almost stiff enough to be a replica of my ex.

For whatever reason, Drunk Me must have thought it would be a brilliant idea to pull the mannequin out from the corner of the room and set him up to watch over me as I slept. I cursed, shambled around the statue, and stomped up the stairs.

I'd slept in my clothes and still had my wallet in my pocket, so after relieving myself and splashing water over my face, I decided it would be less painful to go outside than hide in the cramped, dusty basement. I went to one of my favorite local cafés. There was a corner with dim lighting, and the servers knew me well enough that they wouldn't pester me too often, so I hunkered down to drink coffee and wait out my hangover.

By the time I felt like a human being again, I was late for a university lecture I couldn't miss and had to jog to get there on time. Afterward, Tony invited me to tag along for dinner at a barbecue one of his work friends was throwing. In the end, I didn't get back to Geoff's house until late that night. When I opened the basement door, I was surprised to see the mannequin standing beside the rocking chair under the window.

I paused in the doorway, confused and alarmed, until I realized Geoff must have moved it. When he hadn't seen me that morning, he'd probably come downstairs to check on me and found the mannequin poised above my bed. It must have confused him and likely disturbed him a little, so he'd moved it.

Great. Now he thinks I put the mannequin there on purpose. Talk about making a first impression.

I sighed and half-heartedly kicked my bedsheets back into an approximation of where they should have been then flopped on top of them. When I split from my ex, I'd left just about everything I owned at our apartment—including my clothes, my laptop, and my textbooks. I would need to ask for them back soon, but I dreaded having to carry them the twenty minutes from her apartment to my new basement. I supposed I could ask Tony for help—he was a solid friend and would brave my ex with me like a champ—but I was still holding out for slightly nicer, less-cramped accommodations, preferably without a mannequin.

I rolled over to look at the ceramic figure. He stood beside the rocking chair, his arms hung limp by his sides, and his face was turned to observe the door. His sightless gaze was disquieting, even when he wasn't looking at me.

Sighing, I got up, approached the mannequin, and gripped its arms. The fake skin was colder than I'd expected, almost as if he'd been sitting in a fridge. I shuddered, ground my teeth, tightened my grip on the muscular biceps, and began dragging the statue back toward the corner.

It was heavier than I'd expected, and I was winded by the time I reached the crates and boxes blocking me from his corner. It was incredible that Drunk Me had managed to pull him out the night before.

I looked at the boxes, judged them to be too numerous and heavy to struggle through, and decided it would be easier to leave the mannequin on my side of them. I pushed him into a gap between two boxes, turned him to face the corner, and borrowed the cloth from on top of the mahogany wardrobe to drape over him. When I was done, it was almost possible to pretend he wasn't there at all.

I went upstairs to brush my teeth, shower, and check for messages on my phone. When I got back into the basement, I barely spared a glance at my cloth-covered companion before sliding into bed. I rolled over to face the window and lay there for almost an hour before sleep finally claimed me.

My dreams were disjointed. I imagined I was in university, taking an exam I hadn't studied for. Whenever I looked at the words, they squiggled across the page like worms and resettled in new places to form completely different questions. A tall, dark man with a smooth face stood beside me while I struggled to erase an incorrect answer, and as I watched the words writhe across the pages again, he bent down to whisper in my ear, "Close your eyes."

I sat up with a jolt. Pale light filtered through the window, telling me it was morning. I fumbled for my phone on the bedside table. The clock on my phone confirmed it was just after seven, so I got up and searched for fresh clothes on the coatrack.

I only had three shirts and two pairs of pants, and they were all grimy with settled dust. Grumbling, I shook one of the shirts and a pair of pants, sending plumes of tiny hairs and specks swirling in the early-morning light, then pulled on the clothes.

As I made for the door, I shot a glance at the mannequin. It was no longer where I'd left it, between the boxes. I froze then rotated slowly, my eyes skimming the room.

It wasn't hard to find him. He was posed directly behind the head of the bed, staring down at where I'd been lying just a few minutes before.

A stifled laugh spilled out of me. I glanced around the room, searching for some explanation—and failing to find one. The mannequin stood, legs spread on his stand, his bald head tilted downward. His abs caught a hint of shine from the window's light.

I jumped through the doorway, slammed the door behind me, then jogged up the stairs. The house was quiet; Geoff probably wasn't awake yet. I let myself out through the front door, slung the backpack over my shoulders, and jogged down the near-empty street toward my favorite café.

I stayed there for several hours, stirring a cold mug of coffee and trying not to think about the statue in my new home. I needed someone to talk to who would listen patiently, wouldn't think I was crazy or stupid, and could give me solid advice.

Well, Tony can do two out of three.

Just before the lunch crowd started filtering in, I paid my bill then took the subway to Tony's neighborhood. It was a neglected part of town, but the occasional windowsill potted plant and a small park stopped it from being depressing. I let myself into Tony's apartment complex, climbed the three flights of stairs, and knocked on his door.

He was home, luckily, though he looked as though he hadn't been awake for long. His round, oily face split into a huge grin when he saw me, and he pulled me into his cluttered two-room apartment.

"How you doing, man?" He shoved a pile of clothes off his couch and waved me into the newly freed space. Then before I could answer, he asked, "Want a beer?"

I certainly did, and he fished two bottles out of his fridge. As I opened my beer, he sat next to me and fixed me with his brilliantly carefree smile. "What brings you here on such a lovely day?"

I took a gulp while I tried to think how to phrase my problem. Even Tony, who fervently believed in the Loch Ness Monster, had limits to what he would swallow. I settled on a vague answer: "Something weird is happening in my new apartment."

"What, like with the house owner?"

"No, no, he's fine." Things suddenly fell into place, and I felt acutely stupid for not seeing it sooner.

An explanation—the only possible explanation, really—for the moving mannequin was Geoff. He'd come down to the basement while I was asleep and put the statue behind my bed as a prank. It was a weird thing for him to do, and it definitely pushed the boundaries of personal space. Still, that was less disturbing than imagining the mannequin was sentient. I snorted and gulped down another bitter mouthful of beer. "You know what? It's nothing. Don't worry about it, man."

Tony shrugged and turned the TV on. He was quickly absorbed in a soccer match, and I let my mind wander.

Geoff had seemed like a jovial person when I'd met him. He was probably waiting for me to bound up the stairs, screaming about walking mannequins so he could slap my back and have a laugh at my expense.

Well, that wasn't going to happen. I loved a good prank, but the mannequin was just too creepy to tolerate. When I got back, I would have to confront Geoff and ask him not to move the statue again.

I didn't follow soccer, but Tony did, and it was an easy, distracting two hours. Tony kept fishing more beers from the fridge, and around midafternoon, he phoned for a pizza.

When I left Tony's house shortly after sundown, I was slightly drunk and much less anxious than I'd been that morning. The air was cool and smelled like rain was on the way. I took my time walking home, taking detours through the nicer parts of town to prolong my freedom before retreating to the basement.

When Geoff's house came in sight, I hesitated then quickened my steps. The two-story house stood out like a beacon. Every light in the place was turned on, and the front door stood open, spilling a rectangle of gold down the steps and onto the sidewalk.

I stopped in the doorway and listened to the heavy steps thundering through the back of the house. A moment later, Geoff rounded the corner, his large face beet red from exertion, carrying a suitcase in each hand. He saw me and let his breath out in a rush.

"You're back! Good, good…I was going to write you a note…"

He dropped his suitcases beside the door, wiped the back of his hand across his damp forehead, and gazed about the room. His watery eyes scanned the stack of mail on the narrow hallway table and the phone on the wall.

"Did something happen?" I asked, eyeing Geoff's suitcases warily. *If he's leaving, does that mean I need to find a new place to stay?*

Geoff caught my gaze and gave me a grim smile. "Don't worry. I'm not kicking you out. I've got to be out of state for a couple of days, lad. I'm sorry to do this so soon after you've moved in. It's my sister. She's had a fall, and I...I need to be there for her."

He pulled a handkerchief from his pocket and rubbed it over the rivulets of sweat slipping down his face, his eyes again scanning the room. "I don't think I've forgotten anything... You can use whatever's in the fridge, if you like, so it doesn't go off. The bills are all paid, so no worries there..."

"I'm sorry about your sister," I said, but Geoff didn't seem to hear me.

A taxi honked from the street, and he grabbed his travel cases.

"That's for me, lad. Got to go. I'll call if I'm going to be away for more than a few days. Take care now."

He barreled past me, dragging his suitcases toward the waiting taxi. I closed the door behind him then watched through the curtained windows until the car disappeared.

Geoff had left the lights on in the house, so I went through each room, turning them off. He must have only just gotten the call. A mess of clothes littered the floor around his closet, and he'd left the bathroom cabinets open after collecting his toiletries.

The offer of free food was too tempting to pass up, so I grabbed some leftover chicken and a soda from the fridge for my dinner. I took a shower—much longer than I would have dared if Geoff had been in the house—changed into a pair of my clean clothes, and plugged in my phone. Then I allowed myself the luxury of watching TV in the living room until tiredness started to gnaw at me.

It was getting close to midnight when I made my way down the stairs into the chilly basement. I didn't think Geoff would mind me using the rest of his house while he was gone, but it wouldn't feel right to sleep in his bed, no matter how inviting it was compared to my stiff mattress and dusty concrete room.

The mannequin stood where I'd left him, poised over the head of my bed. I closed the door behind myself, dropped my bag beside the coatrack, and picked the mannequin's discarded cloth off the floor. I threw it over his head, blocking his horrible, blank profile from my sight, then dragged him back to his proper place, wedged between two boxes near the opposite side of the room.

"Looks like it's just you and me for a few days," I said grimly, patting the mannequin's covered head. "Lovely."

I turned the light off and stood by the door for a moment, letting my eyes adjust to the darkness. The rectangular window set high in the wall let in just enough moonlight to guide me back to my bed. I kicked off my shoes and crawled under the sheets, shuddering at how unexpectedly cold they were.

The rooms upstairs had felt so warm and comfortable that it had been easy to become drowsy, but back in my basement, the tiredness melted away. I lay on my back, frustrated and alert, my eyes seeking out patterns in the stained concrete ceiling while the weak moonlight gradually eroded shadows and built new ones in their place.

You've got to get some sleep, I thought after checking my phone and seeing it was creeping up on one in the morning. *You've got classes tomorrow, and you really need to pick up your laptop and study books...brave the fiery wrath of the dragon ex...*

I slipped into a thin, unsatisfying sleep, where dreams blended into reality. The light from the window was fading, like a flashlight that was running out of battery, while the mannequin strode past me, his ceramic joins bending unnaturally as his blank eyes bored into the back of my head.

The door gave a soft click, and I jolted into awareness, sitting up and rubbing at my face while I tried to center myself and shake off the dreams.

The noise had been too real—too close—to have been my imagination, so I fumbled for my phone. I swiped it to turn it on then pointed the thin glow of its screen toward the basement door.

A tall, dark man stood there, as still as stone, staring down at me. I stared back, horrified.

My heart was beating in my ears, like a bird trapped in a cage, thrashing its wings against its prison. Not daring to move, I sat in my bed, prepared to dive backward or defend myself the moment the man moved toward me. The stranger, barely visible in the thin light from my phone, had frozen as well. I could feel him watching me, waiting to see what I would do.

His stillness was unnerving, terrifying, and somehow much worse than motion. The seconds stretched out, each one lasting much longer than they had any right to, while we each waited for the other to make the first move. Then a horrible, crazy thought flitted through my head. *What if it isn't an intruder? What if it's the mannequin?*

I glanced to the right, to where the mannequin should have been propped between the boxes. The phone's light was too weak to make out much more than a cloud of shadows, but I thought I caught sight of the cloth pooled on the floor.

Then darkness poured over us.

My phone had slipped into hibernation. A weak, terrified sound escaped my lips, and I swiped the phone again, calling the light back. I looked up.

The mannequin had moved a full two paces toward me in that second of darkness. He was frozen again, poised just shy of the foot of my bed as he loomed over me, his fingers spread by his sides, his blank face angled down at me.

I clambered out of bed, the adrenaline lending my shaking limbs strength, and darted backward, away from the mannequin. I kept my thumb rubbing over the phone's screen, refusing to let it slip back into darkness, as I pointed the screen toward the mannequin like a priest uses his cross to ward off a vampire.

I kept backing away, refusing to take my eyes off the statue's back, until I reached the door. I grabbed for the knob with my free hand and twisted it. It stuck. I pulled harder, pushed, then put my shoulder against the door and shoved it as hard as I could.

He locked you in, a nasty voice in my head whispered. *He's got you trapped.*

"No," I muttered. I stepped away from the door and searched for the plastic box set in the wall. I found the switch and flicked it. Beautiful, sweet light filled the room.

I took a series of short gulps of air as I put my phone back into

164

my pocket. I didn't dare take my eyes off the mannequin, but he hadn't moved since that second of darkness. I returned to the door again and jiggled the handle. It wouldn't budge.

The spare keys were in my jacket pocket. I edged around the perimeter of the room until I reached the coatrack, where I fumbled for my corded jacket. The first pocket was empty. So was the second one. I kept going, turning out every pocket in it, until there was no room left for doubt. The keys were gone.

They'd been there when I'd let myself into the basement the night before. I remembered putting them back in my pocket before taking off the jacket and hanging it up. And if there was no one in the house except for me and...

I stared at the mannequin's muscular back. He wore no clothes and had no pockets. *If he took the keys, what did he do with them?*

The concrete floor was icy cold under my hands as I knelt before the door. There was a gap of nearly an inch between the wood slab and the ground. I spared a glance toward the mannequin to reassure myself he hadn't moved, then I turned my head and looked under the door.

The short hallway leading to the stairs was almost pitch-black, but a thin sliver of light stretched along the ground. I could just barely make out a glitter of silver at the foot of the first stair, offering tantalizing freedom that was impossible to reach.

A crash, a snap, and then the light was gone once again. I scrambled away from the door, stumbled to my feet, and turned to get my back against a wall. The light from the window had faded as the night progressed, making it impossible to see anything except vague hints of shapes. I tugged my phone back out of my pocket, my eyes uselessly scanning the black room, and swiped my mobile on.

The mannequin stood beside the light, barely a foot away from where I'd been kneeling. His body faced the wall, but his head had turned to follow me. He held something white in his hands. I stared for a moment, extending my phone forward to push the weak light toward him. He was holding a crumpled plastic square with severed wires trailing from it. *The light switch.*

"You bastard," I whispered.

The mannequin didn't reply. He was frozen in the beam of my phone, the indents where his eyes belonged gazing at me. Once again, I felt the overwhelming sensation of being examined, as though his fleshless, lifeless eyes could see far more clearly than my mortal ones. I skittered sideways, toward the window, to get out of his gaze.

Panic was building like a knot of cords in my chest, binding my lungs so I couldn't breathe and restricting my limbs so I couldn't move. The waning burst of adrenaline was urging me to do something—flee, fight, just some sort of action!—but my exit was locked, and I would rather have died than touch the monster in the basement.

"That's what you are," I said, backing toward the window, my feet scraping across the dusty floor as I warded him off with the light from my phone. "A monster."

The back of my legs hit the rocking chair, and I let myself slump into it. The rickety legs creaked under my weight, but it didn't break.

My mind scrambled to find a way out, but every choice was a dead end. The window above me was too narrow for a person to fit through, even if I could break it open. My phone had no signal in the basement. The door was too thick and solid to break, and without the keys, I had no hope of unlocking it.

I glanced past the mannequin. If I could find something—a coat hanger, maybe—to slip through the gap under the door, I could probably hook the keys. But that would mean turning my back to the mannequin again. I instinctively knew that was a terrible mistake…while it was dark, at least.

I tilted my head back to gaze at the window above me. It was narrow and had bars like a jail cell's, but it let me see a strip of inky sky pinpricked with stars.

If I could hold him off until dawn, I might just have a chance to retrieve the keys and make a break for it. I looked back at the mannequin. He remained as motionless as a statue, posed by the defunct light bulb, looking the other way.

"Light's your weakness, huh?" I said. "You can't move as long as I can see you."

As usual, there was no reply. I kicked my heels against the ground, sending the rocking chair into a gentle swing. *How long until dawn?* I turned the phone toward myself for a moment. Three in the morning. I had at least two hours until sunrise.

I rotated the phone back to face the room. The mannequin had moved. In the second I'd taken the light off him, he'd dropped the scrunched plastic from his hand and taken a step toward me.

My breath whistled through my lips in a shaky wheeze as we

stared each other down. My first impulse was to move out of his line of vision, as I'd done before, but I stopped myself. I didn't want to show signs of weakness in front of my stalker.

"Maybe this is best," I told the mannequin while the light jittered over his slate-gray face, casting strange shadows about his eyes. "I can watch you, and you can watch me, but no one gets any closer than we are now."

Time dragged by. When my arm began to ache, I switched the phone to my left hand. I didn't dare break the mannequin's gaze, even as the shadows behind him jumped and leaped in my dim light, clamoring to surge forward and engulf me and my inhuman companion. As the air became colder, goose bumps rose on my arms, and mist began to plume in front of my face. A couple of times, I thought I saw tiny puffs of chilled air appear around the mannequin's set mouth and ceramic nose, but it might have been a trick played by the light.

It was easy to lose track of time in the basement. I kept my chair rocking, using the gentle motion to keep me alert. Each time I kicked against the floor, the worn wooden joints whined in protest. I had my eyes trained on the mannequin, watching the shadows around his eyes quiver as the light shifted from the motion, as I willed myself to stay alert.

Then my phone beeped.

I knew that noise, and a rush of frantic horror poured through me. I stopped rocking the chair, letting it come to a halt as my feet hit the ground, and stared at the statue with fresh dread.

The beep was my phone's warning for low batteries.

How didn't I think of this before? It's been on for hours. Of course the battery's going to drain.

My mouth was dry when I swallowed, and I felt a small bead of sweat trickle down my neck. I imagined the light going out, dead beyond my power to summon it back, trapping me in the inky blackness with my inhuman companion. A strangled noise caught in my throat.

Calm down. Think. Where's the charger?

Upstairs, of course, where I'd left it after fueling the phone before bed.

"Damn it," I whispered. "Damn it, damn it, damn it."

My hand shook, and the unsteady light allowed the shadows to creep across the mannequin's shoulders and up his legs. The way the darkness danced made his face look as though it were moving.

How much battery do I have left? How much time?

I eyed the statue, calculating the risk of taking the light off him versus the agony of not knowing how long my battery would last. Then I turned the phone toward myself as quickly as I could.

He was in darkness for less than half a second, but when the light returned to him, he'd taken a long step forward.

"Damn you to hell," I snarled at him.

I had fifteen percent of my battery left. I'd charged it just before bed, so having its light on was sucking its power quickly.

A headache set in to my right temple as I tried to calculate how long that would give me. It was just after five in the morning. *Surely dawn isn't far away.*

169

I remembered a quote, something I'd read in a novel years before, which suddenly felt much more personal. *The game of patience has changed into a game of endurance.*

There was nothing to do but wait and hope. I kicked against the ground again, setting my chair back to rocking.

I divided my attention. I still watched the mannequin, but I couldn't stop myself from flicking my eyes toward the window above my head. I kept expecting the fresh morning light to break through the black, but if anything, it seemed to be getting darker. I struggled against my desire to check the time. Taking the light off the mannequin for even a second would give him the freedom he craved, but the slow crawl of time was agony. When my limbs were trembling from exhaustion and cold and my eyes were bleary from staring into the dim light, I couldn't stand it any longer.

I flipped the phone around to face myself then immediately turned it back on the mannequin. He'd taken another long step forward, halving the distance between us. I recoiled in my chair, and the pained squeals of its dry wood filled the basement.

I'd seen two important things in the moment I'd been able to look at my phone.

First, it was five forty-two in the morning. I couldn't remember what time dawn broke, but I suspected it wasn't long after six. Second, and much more horrifying, my phone's battery was down to the last two percent.

As I held the shaking light toward the mannequin's face, I thought his thin, stern lips looked a little different. Maybe it was the exhaustion or the stress getting to me, but they seemed to have curled into a grim smile.

"No," I said, using both hands to hold the light, to stop my numb fingers from dropping it. "No, don't come any closer. Don't come any closer. Don't come any closer."

I kept the chant up, gasping thin breaths in between and stealing frequent, quick glances at the window, desperate to see any sort of abatement in the smothering darkness. The mannequin, ever still, ever patient, watched me with those intense, eager eyes. I met his gaze, shook my head…and then my light died.

"Here it is," Geoff said, huffing as he unlocked the basement door. "I haven't touched anything since I got back."

Tony followed the wheezing man into the basement, taking in the surroundings in a quick glance. He recognized his friend's jacket and shirts hanging on a coatrack as well as the backpack sitting by the door.

"He didn't take anything?" Tony asked, crossing the room and glancing at the unmade mattress on the floor.

"Not that I can tell," Geoff said, rubbing the back of his hand across his forehead. "Weirdest thing. He cleared out while I was visiting my sister. Didn't write a note or anything. He left the key at the foot of the stairs, though."

Tony stooped to pick up the phone that had been left on the rocking chair. He pressed the power button, but the battery was dead. "Well, if you hear from him, tell him to get in touch with me. Tell him I'm worried, and his professors say he'll fail if he misses any more classes."

Geoff nodded grimly. "D'you want to take his stuff?"

"I guess I'd better."

Tony grabbed the clothes and phone, stuffed them into the backpack, then followed Geoff toward the stairs. At the threshold of the room, he glanced back, searching for any sign of where or why his friend had disappeared. He saw nothing except the unmade mattress on the floor, the stacks of boxes pushed against the walls, the dilapidated rocking chair sitting under the grimy window, and two slate-gray ceramic mannequins standing against the back wall.

AUTHOR'S NOTE

This is the second story I've centered around mannequins. It's a quasi-prequel to "Lights Out," published in *The Haunting of Gillespie House*.

There's a theory that the more human-like something is—without quite being human—the more frightening it is. Dolls, paintings, snowmen, statues, and wax replicas are all mainstays in horror media. As soon as you add human features to something not alive, it becomes fair game for nightmare fuel.

But none of them unnerve me quite like mannequins.

Over the past few years, I've had plenty of opportunities to confront this irrational fear, though I am yet to conquer it. At the time of writing this, I'm sitting in a café in a shopping mall, being stared down by no less than five mannequins in the store opposite. Some of them don't have heads. It doesn't help.

This isn't the first time, and likely won't be the last, that mannequins make an appearance in my writing.

HITCHHIKER

THE SETTING SUN WAS unpleasantly hot on Helen's back. Her car, a decades-old model with more replacement parts than originals, had tapped out halfway through the drive to Surry. The town where Helen's new apartment was waiting was still two hours away.

She was on a long, derelict road flanked by tangles of sickly shrubs and dry weeds. She hadn't seen another car since leaving her own vehicle more than an hour before, and there was still no sign of the next town. The dirt road crested a few kilometers ahead, and Helen prayed she would top the gentle hill and find a sprawling town on the other side, preferably one with a pay phone and a car repair station that catered to customers who were borderline broke.

The insects hidden in the reeds that poked through swampy land sent up a shrill chatter. A long way away, a bird of prey screeched. Helen shifted her bottle of water to her left hand

and rubbed her sweaty right palm on her jeans. She'd kept her burden as light as possible; the bottle of water was vital for the long walk into town, and she'd tucked her wallet and car keys into her pocket. Everything else, including her dead cell phone and the eight large cardboard boxes full of possessions waiting to be unpacked in her new house, were still in the car.

At least I had the forethought to change into walking shoes, Helen thought as she scuffed her sneakers through the long brown grass that crept onto the dirt road.

A low hum made Helen turn. A ute was coming up behind her, sending clouds of gray dust up in its wake. For a moment, Helen entertained the idea of hitchhiking. It would save her a huge amount of time, no small amount of frustration, and probably a few blisters, but she dismissed the idea almost as soon as it came into her head. She'd heard more than enough stories about hitchhikers going missing and their remains turning up months, or even years, later. There'd even been a spate of disappearances around the area she was moving away from. Young women walking home from the train station and waiting for a bus late at night had vanished. The police were urgently seeking any information the public could provide, but the clues were so sparse that they were almost nonexistent.

Helen focused on watching her feet, hoping the owner of the ute wouldn't try to stop for her. As it drew closer, its engine's noise became clearer; the deep grating rattle seemed both unhealthy and unnatural. *Keep your head down. If you show no interest in him, chances are he'll just pass you by.*

The wheels crunched on loose rocks as the vehicle drew up beside her and, to Helen's frustration, slowed to a crawl.

"Found a problem, miss?" a man asked.

Cancer. That's exactly how Uncle Jerry sounded when he had throat cancer.

She made herself look at the vehicle. It was old, almost as old as her own ill-fated car. Except where she'd taken care to keep hers clean and well maintained, the stranger hadn't. Trash littered the front carriage: crumpled cigarette packages, empty brown bottles, plastic bags, wadded receipts that were so discolored Helen thought they must have been sitting there for years, and a used Band-Aid that had been casually discarded on top of the dashboard.

The man behind the wheel matched his car perfectly. Helen guessed him to be around fifty, but he looked much older. Greasy, steel-gray hair hung too long over his wrinkled forehead, and three days' worth of stubble covered his sunken cheeks. He looked sick—the sort of sick from cancer that's progressed too far to be treated. His skin seemed thin, like crepe paper, and his fingernails were long and stained yellow from nicotine.

As he turned to face her properly, Helen felt a pang of shock; his left eye was an intense sky blue, although age and illness had sent red veins and a yellow tinge over the whites. His right eye, however, was opaque. A bump and a slightly darker circle where his iris had once been pointed at an odd angle compared to the other eye, as though it were blindly staring at a space far past Helen's left shoulder.

"I'm fine," Helen said bluntly, averting her eyes. Instead of stopping, she increased her speed as she moved off the dirt road and began marching through the underbrush.

"You sure about that?" the man slurred. "Pretty woman like you shouldn't be walking this road alone."

Helen didn't answer. Her heart was thundering, and her stomach was cold and tight. *Leave me alone. Can't you see I don't want to talk? Just keep driving.*

She was drawing ahead of him, so the man tapped his accelerator to push his ute forward, sending black smoke from the exhaust. Motion just above the dashboard attracted Helen's attention—a trinket hung on the rearview mirror danced around. At first, she thought it was a strange, furry fruit, but then it rotated on its cord and Helen caught sight of a nose, two eyelids sutured closed, and a mouth distorted into a bizarre grimace.

What the hell? He has a shrunken head. A shrunken head in his car. Is it real? She spared a second glance at the tanned, stitched-up skin then looked away again as nausea rose into her throat. *It looks real.*

"This isn't a good road." The man licked his dry lips. His good eye was skimming Helen's body, while the blind eye stared intently at the sky.

"I'm fine," Helen repeated, and her voice sounded very strange and weak in her own ears. She was all but running, but the man in his ute kept abreast of her easily. He was grinning at her, and Helen saw that although he still had the majority of his teeth, many of them were rotting.

A thousand scenarios ran through Helen's mind. *Keep off the road so he can't run you over. Use your keys as a weapon. He's old; you could probably beat him in a fistfight if it came to that.*

Then the man said the one thing Helen had been dreading. "Lots of people go missing on this road, you know."

Heart in throat, bottle of water sloshing in her sweaty hand, Helen started running. The ute's engine revved as it lurched forward to match her pace. The man was saying something to her, but she couldn't hear him over the engine.

Don't turn around. Don't slow down. Don't look at him—

Something hard was digging into Helen's stomach. She rolled backward, trying to escape it, and dry, prickly weeds scratched at her face. She opened her eyes to see the sky filled with dirty twilight.

With a groan, Helen sat up. Her back, arms, and legs ached, almost as though she'd been run over. She pressed her palm to her swimming head, waiting for it to clear.

What happened? Did he—

Suddenly panicked, Helen did a quick mental inventory. Her jeans were still buttoned, and while her back ached and her limbs felt bruised, nothing hurt where it wasn't supposed to. She let her breath out and pushed her loose hair out of her face. *What happened, then?*

She was sitting on the edge of the dirt road, in almost the same spot she'd been before she blacked out. The gnarled tree to her left looked familiar.

The twilight didn't seem to have deepened much, either. Shapes melted together and played tricks on her eyes. Insects were chattering in the weeds beside her, and a bird of prey cried out in the distance. The ute and its repulsive occupant were nowhere to be seen.

Get into town. Find somewhere with a lot of people. You can worry about everyone else once you're somewhere safe.

Helen's legs felt unsteady as she pushed herself to her feet. She stretched, felt the bruises along her arm flare, then started walking. When her sneaker hit something solid, she looked down, surprised to see the bottle of water lying barely a foot from where she'd been left. She picked it up then remembered about her wallet and keys. Both were still in her pocket.

If he didn't assault me or rob me, what exactly did he do?

Helen unscrewed the bottle of water and took a deep drink. Then she started walking again, suddenly wanting to reach the town more than she'd wanted anything in her life. *Maybe I'll splurge on a hotel room and wait until morning before continuing the drive.*

Then she heard the rumble of another approaching car. The reaction was immediate; her heart rate rose, and a sheen of sweat covered her body as her adrenaline prepared her to respond to the threat.

Relax. It's just a car. Not every human on this planet is dangerous. Keep your head down, and it'll pass you by.

She couldn't stop her reaction to the noise, though. Fear

clotted in her chest and left a metallic taste in her mouth as she increased her pace to a jog. The roar of the engine felt familiar; it had a rattle and unnatural cadence similar to the man's ute. Almost...*exactly* the same.

Helen glanced over her shoulder, and the fear, previously just a whisper in her ear, commandeered her body. The ute, its dashboard littered with long-empty cigarette cases and beer bottles, was gaining on her quickly. Its shrunken head bobbed and danced on the string as its owner's sallow, diseased face watched Helen.

The bottle of water fell from Helen's hand. She was running, dragging in terrified breaths. Squeezing her eyes shut against the image, she prayed she was going crazy and that it was all in her mind.

He's come back for me. Come back to finish the job. He'll skin me, probably, turn my face into a new shrunken head so I can bob along beside his other trinket for the rest of eternity—

"Found a problem, miss?" the man crowed at her as the ute's engine roared.

This time, the rock was digging into her back. Helen gasped, feeling disoriented as she rolled onto her hands and knees. The dizziness had returned, and the bruises on her limbs made her shudder. She lurched into a sitting position and waited for the ache in her head to clear.

He came back for me. Why? What for? Did he run me over with his ute? It would explain why everything hurts…

But it didn't explain why she was still alive. If she'd really been hit by the ute going at that speed, she would have broken bones and serious internal damage at the very least.

Helen rubbed her hair out of her eyes and looked around. She was still on the same stretch of road, with the same twisted black tree sticking out of the reeds to her left. The insects were humming; above her, a bird of prey gave a loud cry.

This feels so familiar. Like déjà vu.

Helen scanned the ground and saw the bottle of water lying there, waiting for her. She picked it up and swirled it around, confused by what she saw. It was half-full. *Didn't I drink most of it earlier?*

She looked at the sky. It was still twilight, hovering in that indefinite time that never lasted more than a handful of minutes.

Don't go there, Helen told herself as she unscrewed the bottle of water and took a drink. *Don't you dare start thinking about time travel.*

But what if? the other, more adventurous half of her mind asked.

Don't start asking what-ifs. The last thing we want is to see that damn ute again.

She glanced to the right, where the empty road behind her stretched into the distance. She let her breath out in a sigh and massaged her left shoulder, where the bruised muscles were tight. *Something very strange has happened, but you can worry about that after you reach the town. What's important is that you're alive, you've still got all of your limbs attached, and that ute is nowhere to be seen.*

She'd barely gotten to her feet when she heard the rumble of an engine behind her. Dread, icy cold and uncomfortably familiar, filled her chest as she turned around.

The ute was topping the ridge down the road. It was still too far away to see clearly, but she was sure it was the same dirty vehicle. Helen licked her lips, which suddenly seemed very dry.

Should I run? Hide?

Running hadn't helped her before. After two encounters with the ute, she was reluctant to turn her back on it again.

The vehicle was gradually gaining on her, kicking up black dust behind it as it roared down the road. Helen stood her ground, shivering and sweating as stress built in a tight ball inside her. She felt as though she might be sick.

Don't run. Don't let him out of your sight.

Helen carefully pulled her key ring out of her back pocket and gripped it in her fist so that the keys stuck out between her fingers like tiny, blunt blades. The ute had come close enough for her to see its occupant; the grizzled man's face split into a rotten-toothed smile as he met her gaze. The shrunken head bobbed like a Christmas bauble below the mirror.

He slowed down as he drew closer and eventually came to a halt right beside her. Helen was close enough to smell the ute, which stank of beer, cigarette smoke, and urine.

"Found a problem, miss?" the man asked for the third time that day.

"I don't know," Helen said, choosing her words carefully. Her hand holding her keys was hidden behind her back, and her muscles were tense as she prepared to lunge and attack at a second's notice if the man made a move toward her.

"Pretty woman like you shouldn't be walking this road alone." He tilted his head back to scratch at his stubble with yellowed nails. His good eye roved over her as though assessing her for the first time, while his blind eye watched the slowly rotating shrunken head.

Helen hesitated. She wasn't sure if she should tell him about her broken car, but she guessed he must have passed it and would have put two and two together already.

"This isn't a good road," the man continued when Helen didn't speak. "Lots of people go missing 'round here."

"Why?" Helen asked, surprised by her own boldness. Her nerves had been charged with electricity; she shifted from foot to foot, intensely uncomfortable but determined not to show her fear.

The man regarded her for a moment, head cocked to one side, dry lips pursed. Then he said, "You've not long left Carlton's border. If you continue up the road a little way, you'll be in Mellowkee. But here, this little patch of road, is Harob land. You heard of Harob before, miss?"

"No." Helen couldn't guess where he was going. The twilight was gradually fading into true night, and the insects behind her had quietened.

"Not many people have." The man scratched at his grizzled chin again. "'Cept, of course, for the souls who live there. I suppose most folks want to forget it exists. Strange things happen in Harob. Things that might give you and me some trouble sleeping at night. If you find yourself in Harob country, you're best if you move on as quick as you can."

Helen shook her head slowly, indicating that she didn't understand what he was implying. The man reached forward, digging through the litter on the passenger seat, and Helen reflexively took a half step back. He was only searching for a cigarette box, though, and when he'd found one that wasn't empty, he pulled out one of the rolls and clamped it between his cracked lips.

"A more immediate concern for you, at least, is the sinkholes." He cupped one hand around the cigarette as he lit it, then took a long drag and blew the smoke out of the open windows. It occurred to Helen that the shrunken head might not have been that brown when the man had bought it. "Lots of sinkholes around here. They're hard to see in the day, and even harder at night. You'll want to be careful."

"Okay." Helen shifted uneasily and glanced at the road to her left, where she could still see the lip of the ridge, silhouetted in the fading light. "How far's the next town?"

"Augh, it'd have to be—what? Twenty minutes' drive." Another puff of smoke, then he raised his eyebrows at her. "Want a lift?"

"No. But thank you for offering."

Again, his single working eye roved over her, assessing her dirty sneakers, jeans, light cardigan, and near-empty bottle of water. "You sure about that? It'll be a bit of a hike for a little lady like you."

"I'm sure." Helen put as much force into her voice as she could and managed to flash him a tight smile. "Completely sure."

"Suit yourself." He moved the cigarette to the other side of his mouth and turned back to the steering wheel. "Watch out for those sinkholes, now. They're hard to see."

"I will."

The sound of the ute's revving engine grated at Helen's nerves, and the vehicle picked up speed as it followed the road toward the ridge. Helen watched it until it disappeared, then she let her breath out and sagged.

She wasn't dead, kidnapped, skinned, or any of the other terrible possibilities she'd been preparing for. If the man had been telling the truth, the town would still be a few hours' walk away, but that was bearable. Helen drained her bottle then screwed its cap back on and began following the road.

The sounds had changed. With the end of daylight and the emergence of a smattering of weak stars, new insects had started a shrill song. An owl called from behind her, and one of its companions to her right answered. Helen had to slow her pace and focus on where she was walking to make sure she didn't step on a loose stone and twist her ankle.

There was a strange, dark patch in the ground ahead of her, mingling with the weeds and pressing against the side of the road. It looked like a shadow, but there was nothing to cast it. Helen had to crouch down in front of it before she recognized what it was: a hole. Plants and vines grew so heavily around its edge that it was almost perfectly camouflaged in the bad light. It was at least two meters wide and three meters long. Helen leaned over its edge to see how far down it went, but she couldn't see for more than a few feet.

Watch out for those sinkholes, now.

The water bottle was empty and would have been just useless luggage for the rest of her walk. Helen dropped it into the hole and listened to the hollow tap as it hit the sides again…and again…and again, before fading from her hearing.

"Damn," Helen muttered, sitting back on her haunches. The old man had been right; sinkholes like this were a hazard for anyone walking the roads in poor light—or anyone who wasn't paying attention to the road, for that matter.

Helen glanced behind herself, to the spot where the ute had pulled alongside her. She'd been running in this direction, keeping off the road so that the ute couldn't easily hit her. It was a miracle she hadn't fallen into the sinkhole.

Suddenly uneasy, Helen stood up. She had barely a second to realize the ground was shifting under her feet, collapsing as the ledge she hadn't realized she was standing on crumbled, and then—

The rock was poking into her shoulder. Helen groaned. Her whole body ached as though she'd been hit by a truck…or fallen down a very steep incline.

She sat up slowly, waiting for the dizziness to pass. The light was fading as twilight converted day into night. To her left was the grizzled tree poking out of the marshes. Helen put her hand out to where she already knew her bottle would be and picked it up, feeling the water slosh inside it.

This can't be happening.

She sat where she was for a long time, waiting for the aches to ease as she listened to the hiss of insects and the bird of prey's single call. When she saw the ute top the ridge farther down the road, she carefully got to her feet, brushing her hands over her jeans to clean off the worst of the dust.

The ute pulled up beside her, and its haggard occupant focused his one good eye on her. "Found a problem, miss?"

Helen hesitated only for a second before answering. "Yes, actually. Can I get a ride into town?"

He gazed at her for a moment, taking her measure, before saying, "Sure thing. Hop in."

She opened the door and waited for him to scoop the litter off the passenger seat. The shrunken head rotated slowly until its stitched-closed eyes were facing Helen, then it continued to turn to survey the road. Helen climbed into the ute and pulled on her seat belt.

"Where're you heading to?"

"Town," Helen said simply, watching as the twilight gradually eased the landscape into darkness, her half-full water bottle clasped in her lap with both hands. "As quickly as you can, please."

"Sure thing, miss." The man pressed down on the accelerator, and the vehicle ground forward, its engine's noise rattling at Helen's nerves. "Best to move through this part of the country as quick as you can, anyhow."

AUTHOR'S NOTE

Living in Australia, a continent with daunting gaps between towns and patchy public transport, I've always been aware of my country's history of hitchhiking-related disappearances. The most famous are the Backpacker Murders, where at least seven young adults were killed by Ivan Milat and hidden in the Belanglo State Forest, not far from my home. The part of the forest that faces the highway is a pine plantation with lovely even rows of trees. They look peaceful and tidy, no different from any other plantation, but it's impossible to pass them without thinking about what happened in the scrubbier, untended areas beyond.

This short story plays into the dangers of hitchhiking but takes a different turn: What if a hitchhiker was cautious, and what if their caution was justified, but it was directed toward the wrong recipient?

BELLAMY

"HELLO, BELLAMY," LEANNE WHISPERED and turned off her car. As the engine's rumbling faded, she began to hear the crickets and creaking trees filtering through the early evening.

The cloistered building waited ahead. It sprawled between the trees, seeming to absorb the entire horizon. The failing sun painted its edges a bloody red as endless black windows watched the empty courtyard.

The exterior was flat and grim, more like a warehouse than a home. But Leanne knew, inside, Bellamy Children's Asylum was far from orderly. A nest of discordant passageways and connecting rooms created maddening patterns. Nothing fit the way it was intended. What should have been right angles weren't, and floors and ceilings that should have been flat were bent. Even after living in the home for eight months, Leanne still didn't know where some of the passageways led.

Why did you leave me, Leanne?

She pressed her eyes closed, hands tight on the wheel, and waited for the painful sensation in her chest to fade. Thirty years should have been long enough to forget the home. Thirty years should have been long enough for the dreams to stop.

Her car door whined as she opened it. The car wasn't old, but it seemed to resent the twelve-hour drive. Leanne flexed her shoulders as she stepped onto the pebbles of the parking area. Once, those pebbles had been like a white carpet spread before the building. Now, they were a deep, angry gray, buried under the residue of generations of weeds.

Leanne and Henry had been some of the last children brought into Bellamy. Since then, times had changed. Children's asylums had lost favor, and foster homes had replaced them. Two years after Leanne left the home, it had closed its doors for the last time. Evidently, no one had been interested in purchasing it. The building was dirtier and held more cracks than Leanne remembered, but otherwise, it looked exactly as she remembered.

I waited for you, Leanne.

She took a slow breath, removed the flashlight from her pocket, and climbed toward the front door. It had been left ajar, perhaps by human error or age and wind had forced it open. Leanne tried to push the gap wider, but the wood was frozen in place. The gap was just large enough to squeeze through. She turned her body sideways and slipped inside.

Leanne paused, waiting to see if her eyes would adjust. Tinted

BELLAMY

daylight came through the door's gap, creating a streak that ran across the floor before fading into the gloom. But not before it caught on two wide eyes.

Her pulse leaped. She raised the flashlight, fingers turning sweaty as she pressed the button. The corner of the room came into relief. The eyes vanished, resolving into a brass fixture. That was all.

She turned the flashlight in a slow arc, revealing what remained of the building she had once called home. It was sparsely furnished, as it had been during her time there. The bronze fixtures and broken chandelier whispered of an earlier era when the home had been grand. But the chairs and cupboards were severe and unadorned, additions from an owner with less money to spare. There were no bottles or graffiti and no signs that anything had been stolen. No vandals. Bellamy had likely been forgotten by everyone who had not lived there.

Leanne's flashlight caught on a pair of bronze door handles. She approached, her shoes crunching in the dust and dead insects coating the floor. The bronze, tarnished and almost black, was painfully familiar. Leanne pressed on one of the handles. It left a dark smear across her palm, but the door groaned inward, welcoming her into the dining hall.

The massive wooden table ran the length of the room. Forty chairs crowded around it. Leanne could picture Grace, the younger warden, standing by a pot near the room's corner and ladling soup into the children's bowls as they approached, single file. Leanne had liked Grace. Pretty, with delicate fingers, like a

197

fairy, she was the one bright spot in the house. She never yelled and gave generous servings. When she spoke, which wasn't often, it was gentle and affectionate.

Leanne remembered wishing she could ask Grace to sing her a song to lull her to sleep, just like her mother used to. But there were forty children living in the home, too many for one woman to lavish with affection, no matter how hard she tried. And Grace had been sickly. Some days, shivering and her pale face speckled with sweat, she had not even been able to rise out of her chair. On those days, Patience served the meals.

No one had seemed to know their relationship—whether they were simply friends or mother and daughter. They had been so different that it was hard to imagine they could be related. Grace was young and with hair so light it was almost gold. Patience was tall, with black hair tied back from her severe face. She walked with a cane, and the hard tapping noise could be heard long before she came into sight. Leanne had hated the noise…almost as much as she'd hated the eyes.

What a woman to leave in charge of children.

Without even realizing it, Leanne had approached the seat she always sat on. Her fingers traced over the top, feeling the hard wood under the dust, then she pulled out the chair. As she sank into it, the memories felt so close they were almost real.

"I wish she'd leave us alone," Henry whispered.

No one at the table spoke loudly. No one wanted their voice to be the one that stood out. Patience stalked around the gathering, her cane clicking on the stone floor with every step. Her face could have been made of stone. The cold expression stayed fixed, unemotional, save for her eyes, which moved in short little jolts, flicking from bowed head to bowed head. A milky white sheen covered the irises, like blind eyes, except nothing escaped her notice. Leanne hated those eyes.

"She's old," Leanne whispered back. "Maybe she'll die soon."

The eyes swiveled toward her. The pupils stared through the sheen. A chill coursed through Leanne. She bowed her head, trying to escape those horrible eyes, her throat tight and her stomach squirming. Patience couldn't have heard. She'd been careful to keep her voice soft. And yet, the clicking noise was moving closer, louder, and she could still feel the eyes on her, unblinking...

A touch of ice ran across Leanne's shoulder. Cold, ephemeral, the sensation was both there and not. A dead finger, tracing her skin. She staggered out of the seat, knocking it over. The flashlight's beam shook as it raced across the walls and floor. She was alone.

Leanne reached her spare hand up to touch her shoulder. It was wet. She held the fingers ahead of herself, rubbing the liquid between them, then turned the flashlight upward. A dark stain, wider than Leanne's arm reach, marred the ceiling. The roof had a leak.

She breathed deeply as she backed away from the table. Her breath misted. She wished she'd brought a heavier jacket.

I miss you, Leanne.

There was a purpose for her visit. She wasn't there just to call up old memories. Leanne brushed her hand across her cheek, wiping off a smear of perspiration that had formed despite the cold, and turned toward a door behind her.

In the kitchen beyond it, the old pots still sat on the stoves. Leanne looked into one. The skeletal remains of a mouse were nestled among the dust. The space was too cluttered for her light to do more than confuse it with running shadows, but Leanne knew the kitchens well. Bellamy had survived on donations from the public, and there was barely enough money for food, let alone staff. It was run entirely by Patience and Grace. The children were expected to help with chores; the girls did the cooking, and the boys cleaned. Leanne hadn't liked those hours. She could sneak little scraps of food—the ends of carrots or sometimes even a sliver of cheese—but being in the kitchen separated her from Henry.

Through the back door, Leanne entered the main part of the house. The hallways were narrower than she remembered. She supposed, as a child, she had fit better. As an adult, she felt squeezed. She had to walk perfectly straight. Otherwise, one of her shoulders would scrape the discolored plaster.

The hallway bent. It was not at a right angle. It wasn't far off—only ten degrees, perhaps—but it left Leanne feeling destabilized. She hadn't questioned it as a child, but as an adult, she couldn't make sense of it. The rooms were all rectangular. How did the hallways have the luxury of variation?

A memory returned. On the days Patience went to town, the children would play hide-and-seek through the halls. One child would wait at the window overlooking the yard, prepared to call a warning in case Patience returned. The others ran through the building, finding nooks and secret holes to tuck themselves into. As children were uncovered, they joined the search. No matter how often the game was played, they never seemed to run out of new places to hide.

Leanne's hand brushed a cupboard set into the wall. She thought she remembered using it for one of the games. Cautiously, she pulled on the handle. Inside were shelves of crumbling, moth-eaten blankets. A storage space had been left empty below. Leanne glanced down the hallway, as though she were at risk of being seen, then bit her lip as she got to her hands and knees.

She wasn't as young or as small as she had once been, and her joints creaked as she fit herself into the narrow gap. She remembered it. As she pulled the door closed, the sensations of that winter afternoon rushed back.

She had been hiding for ages. Maybe half an hour. They still hadn't found her. Leanne rested her chin on her knees, waiting, and feeling faintly pleased.

For a while, footsteps had thundered through the hallways, voices whispering suggestions as they tried to find the remaining hiders. Shadows had flitted across the band of light at the base of the door. The footsteps had faded, though, and she couldn't hear them any longer. She couldn't hear anything…except the quiet tap of a cane.

Leanne clamped a hand over her mouth. Patience was home. She hadn't heard the warning. She hadn't gotten out in time.

The tapping, a deep, steady noise, was growing closer. Louder.

Matching the beating of Leanne's heart. A shadow moved across the gap at the base of the floor. The cane thudded for a final time, loud enough to echo. The silence was agony. The shadow didn't move.

Leanne raised her second hand to cover her mouth. She was cold all of a sudden. So desperately cold that she wanted to gasp. She closed her eyes, squeezing them, as though she could escape Patience in the black inside her head.

The cupboard's handle rattled. Then it began to turn.

A cold, sharp tapping noise broke through Leanne's memory. For an instant, she felt the same chill that had haunted her as a child. The dread, the fear, the need to run. She scrambled out of the hole in the cupboard and stopped, gasping, on her hands and knees in the hallway.

The tapping came again. It was too fast and too light, she realized. Patience's cane had been deep, almost thudding. This was the sound of a branch tapping on glass.

She rose to her knees and looked along the hallway. At its end, a window framed dead branches that bowed in the wind. She did not remember the window being there when she'd first started along that hall.

A hint of embarrassment brought heat to Leanne's cheeks. She stood, her legs unsteady, and leaned a hand against the wall. It had been thirty years. Patience was long gone.

She briefly wondered what had happened to Grace. She'd never known the woman's surname. Leanne hoped she'd lived a good life after the home closed, but her heart sunk as she realized that was not likely. Grace's health had been poor. Leanne imagined she could still hear the coughing, soft and weak, that seemed almost incessant on Grace's worse days.

The hallway led deeper into the building. Leanne let it carry her around another bend, then took an offshoot. She couldn't remember where the path led. After a moment, it ended in one of the narrow, angled wooden staircases that seemed to fill the home. Leanne pulled her jacket tighter, trying to fight off the pervasive cold, and began to climb.

"What's wrong, sweetheart?"

She'd been hiding in the staircase, crying. She'd thought it was near the back of the house, where no one would find her, but somehow, Grace had. The woman crouched on the step below her and took Leanne's hands in hers. Grace's fingers always seemed to tremble, even though she was never afraid. She rubbed Leanne's hands and smiled up at her.

"We were playing hide-and-seek yesterday." Leanne heaved, fresh tears falling over her cheeks. "I know we aren't supposed to, but we did."

"That's all right, sweetheart. You're not in trouble. I promise." Grace's smile was warm. Like sunlight. The rest of the house was so cold, but Grace seemed to make it more bearable.

"But-but I can't find Andrew." Leanne shook her head. Her hair was sticking to her wet cheeks. Mucus ran from her nose. She wanted to wipe it away, but she didn't want to take her hands out of Grace's. "He went to hide, but after the game ended, I didn't see him for the rest of the day, and now, today, he wasn't at breakfast, either. What if he's still lost? What if he's stuck somewhere and can't get out?"

"Well now, that's something I'll take care of." Her voice was comforting, full of quiet certainty. "He won't have just disappeared. I'll find him. Here."

Grace slipped something small and gem-green out of her pocket. Cellophane crinkled as she placed the sweet in Leanne's hand.

"A little treat." Grace's thumb brushed over Leanne's cheek, wiping away the moisture. "Don't tell Patience I gave it to you, though, all right? It will be our secret."

"Promise."

"Good girl. Now, go and wash your face. Your class will be start-ing soon. I want you to be very brave and try not to worry. I'll take care of it all."

As Leanne climbed the stairs toward the bathroom, she glanced back at Grace. The woman stared into the distance. Strands of delicate golden hair caught the light, making her seem to almost glow. Her words had been comforting. But now that she thought Leanne was no longer watching, she had let her smile fall. A worried crease ran between her eyes.

Leanne stopped, her hand resting on the wall at the top of the stairs. She'd forgotten all about that day. She frowned, staring into the dusty gloom ahead, trying to recall the aftermath, whether Andrew had been found. Leanne could picture his face, pinched and gap-toothed, but she didn't remember seeing him again after that game of hide-and-seek.

Cold prickles ran across her back. She lifted the flashlight and used it to disperse some of the darkness. The hall went on seemingly forever, doors recessed into each side. She recognized them. The classrooms.

After breakfast, they'd always gone to study. The children were divided by age, eight or ten to a room, and Grace went between them, passing out old, tattered books and instructing them on which passages to read.

Leanne and Henry were twins and allowed to sit next to each other. They would pull their seats close, sharing a book. Leanne turned the pages since Henry was the faster reader.

They were left alone for long stretches of a time in those classrooms. They always worked dutifully and silently. Not because they wanted to, but because the doors were left open, and Patience walked the hallway.

Leanne remembered feeling the eyes on her every time the heavy cane passed their door. She kept her head down to their book, desperate to avoid notice. When Patience passed, the rooms fell deathly still. No one fidgeted. No one whispered or turned their pages or even breathed. She would linger in the doorway, those milky eyes seeing everything, before the thud of her cane announced her progress toward the next room. Then the children would have a few minutes of peace before the cane returned.

One afternoon, after the incident at breakfast, Henry had leaned toward Leanne and whispered, "I hope she dies soon." She'd giggled, pressing a hand across her lips to stifle the noise because the cane was still not out of earshot.

Leanne sighed, leaning against the doorjamb, staring at the

desks she and Henry had occupied. She remembered the rooms being bigger. A child's eyes had the power to magnify things. Even the windows had felt far wider and more alluring when she was a girl. Back then, they had tried to call Leanne away from her desk, to lure her into risking Patience's notice for a glimpse outside. Now, as an adult, they seemed narrow and sad.

Leanne approached one and stared through it. The sun had gone down. Soon, the moon would illuminate the world below. She could barely make out the trees and bushes that had grown behind Bellamy.

Their mornings were spent in the classrooms. Their afternoons were for chores: cooking, washing clothes, making beds, and sweeping floors. Then they had dinner. And after that, they had a brief few hours to themselves, which they always spent outside. It was the best part of the day, racing through the long grass and chasing rabbits around the forest's edge. The bell would ring at eight o'clock sharp, and they would all file back inside under Patience's glazed eyes.

"Jayne!" Leanne cupped her hands around her mouth. "Jayne, come back! It's too late!"

Jayne laughed as she frolicked through the grass and leaped over a rotting log. "It'll only be a minute, silly!"

Leanne sighed and threw her hands out to her side. Henry appeared next to her, holding a stick he had been using to hunt for frogs. He looked at her curiously.

"She says she's going down to the river to wade," Leanne said.

"But it's too late. The bell's going to ring any moment, and she'll be in trouble if she can't get back fast enough."

A vivid sunset streaked across the sky. The days had been growing longer, the sun lingering, and the bell seemed to come earlier every evening.

"Well, that's her problem." Henry swiped his stick through the grass. "I heard we're going to get a new one tomorrow. I hope they're not going to be put in our room. They'd need to add a new bed, and there's no space as it is."

Leanne didn't mind having more bodies sharing their bedroom. At night, when she lay awake, the gentle breathing and rustling of sheets was a comfort. More than anything, she was afraid of being alone, especially when the thudding cane passed along the hallway.

The bell chimed, deep, angry booms that seemed to jangle her bones and ring through her skull. Leanne looked toward the tree line. Jayne was out of sight.

"She's going to be in trouble," she repeated and turned to run after Henry as he beckoned her toward the door.

Children emerged from all areas of the yard, some brushing grass out of their clothes, others tossing aside sticks and woven toys that were not allowed inside. Patience stood at the door, her back ramrod straight, ringing the bell with steady, long pulls of the rope. Leanne fell to a walk as she filed up the steps. Running was not permitted in Bellamy.

As she passed Patience, she looked over her shoulder. Jayne still had not emerged from the forest. Leanne frowned. She couldn't have gone that far.

The last child passed through the door. Patience stood in the *opening a moment longer, her milky eyes scanning the gathered children. One long arm extended, indicating toward the stairs in a silent instruction to wash and prepare for bed.*

As Leanne climbed toward their rooms, she heard the doors to the yard close and lock with a heavy click. She looked back. She didn't see Jayne. Patience stared at the closed doors, her hands clasped on top of her cane, the knobby knuckles pale in the dim light.

Leanne stepped back from the glass, letting her hand fall to her side. She didn't remember what had happened to Jayne, whether the girl had knocked to be let in, or whether she had been subjected to a punishment. She shook her head. It seemed like something she should remember.

She remembered the new girl who had arrived the following day, though. A tiny, mousy thing with drooping cheeks. As Henry had worried, she'd been put into their bedroom. But they hadn't needed to add an extra bed. There had been one empty and waiting.

"Jayne's bed?" Her lips formed the words, but no sound left. Leanne's throat was dry.

She turned to face the desks. She could picture her schoolmates. Leanne raised a hand and pointed at each desk as she called out their names. "Helen. Poppy. James. Susan. No—that's not right. Paul sat at that desk."

She approached it and ran her fingertips across the wood surface. Paul had sat there. But so had Susan. She'd taken his place once he'd left. "Left to where?"

Bellamy was a children's asylum. It was never intended to be a permanent home. Parents would reclaim the children they had been forced to give up. New families would adopt in an effort to give them a better life. Any unclaimed children would be sent out to find work and their own home once they were old enough. But, as Leanne stared at Paul's desk, she couldn't remember why he had left.

She couldn't remember why *any* of them had left. There had been no scenes of children greeting long-lost relatives. No families had ever been allowed into the home to adopt. There had never been any talk of jobs or leaving. Her last memory of Paul involved him sitting at that very desk.

The cane clicked on the hardwood floor as Patience approached. She paced along that hallway ceaselessly during their studies, watching over all of them.

Leanne could hear the cane coming well before it arrived. It was like a screw in her back, winding her tighter and tighter the nearer it came. She kept her head down, pretending to read a passage on European history in the tattered book she and Henry shared. If she kept still, the cane would pass, the way it always did, and she could breathe freely for another few minutes.

A cackling laugh came from two desks to her right. Paul clamped his hands over his mouth, his shoulders shaking. His desk mate had doodled an image into their workbook. Leanne craned her neck. The drawing depicted Patience; the dark cane was unmistakable. But in this image, Patience's head rolled on the floor.

The tapping was almost upon them. Leanne put her head back down, feigning focus on her book, but through her peripheral vision, she watched Paul. He rushed to flip the page, to hide the crude drawing, but mirth had him in its grip. His back shook, his eyes watered. Both hands were pressed across his mouth as he fought the cackling laughter that wanted to escape.

Patience's tall frame moved into the doorway. Her black hair nearly reached the ceiling. Her shoulders blocked Leanne's view of the hallway beyond. The cane clicked a final time as it was set down in front of her. She stared into the room, her face an expressionless mask.

Paul was trembling. He hunched, head nearly touching the desk. Leanne's stomach turned cold and sick. She stayed so still that her muscles began to ache. There was not a single noise in the rest of the room, not even a drawn breath.

Then a whining giggle escaped between Paul's fingers. Patience lifted her cane. She slammed it into the floor. The single ringing thud made Leanne jolt. Then one of her white-knuckled hands left the wood. It rose and pointed toward Paul, then the fingers turned and beckoned.

Paul was no longer laughing. He kept his hands clamped over his mouth, below two wide, frightened eyes. He turned to look at the rest of them in a silent question, a request for help. They didn't move, not even to raise their heads. Paul finally dropped his hands away from his mouth. His lips had turned white. He stood and slowly, unsteadily walked toward Patience.

His desk-mate reached toward him then thought better of it, putting his head back down. Patience turned and wordlessly began

210

*walking along the hallway. Paul sent them one final plaintive look,
then followed.*

"Oh." Leanne pressed her hand to her throat. She remembered now. She recalled listening to Patience's cane as she left the study hallway and took Paul deeper into Bellamy, beyond where Leanne could hear them. Paul had not returned. The next day, a new girl took his seat.

The boy who had sat beside him—the one who had drawn the image that had made Paul laugh—had become withdrawn after that. He'd no longer made jokes or spoken during their meals. He hadn't done much except sit in the grass during their hours outside. Five days later, his desk was empty as well.

Leanne backed toward the door. She'd forgotten all of that. And it hadn't just been them. There had been others. Her eyes darted across the desks, lips moving to form the names. Stevie, Laura, Mary... She'd met them all during her first day at Bellamy, but a month later, they were gone. Richie had left his bed to go to the bathroom late one night and not returned. Harriett had been sent to fetch more soap while they were washing the windows one afternoon, but they had finished the job without it. Neil was playing a game of tag outside and did not return for the bell. There were so many missing children. Too many. All gone without a whisper.

"How could I forget?"

She knew how—because she had tried to forget. After leaving Bellamy, she had done everything in her power to excise it from her mind. She thought if she could forget, the dreams would stop, as well.

Seeing the building brought it back. The acidic taste of fear that permeated the hallways. The urge to keep her back to a wall. The sense of dread that had come with the sound of that cane.

Leanne was shaking. She wiped her hand across her forehead, feeling the cold sweat there. This visit had been planned to give her closure, to end the nightmares. But all it had done was reopen old wounds.

"Henry." She turned toward the end of the hallway. Behind a door, a set of stairs led to the third floor…and its bedrooms.

Sick dread weighed her legs down. The shivering flashlight beam ran across the narrow walls and brass door handle as Leanne neared it. She didn't want to see more. She didn't want to remember more. But she had to. Without this last step, without knowing what had happened, she would never be able to rest.

The handle, disused for thirty years, didn't want to turn. Leanne fought with it. Her skin ached as it slipped on the metal, but then the latch screeched as it retracted and the door fell open.

These stairs were chaos. They listed to the right then tilted back to the left. Some were shallow, others so narrow that Leanne had to balance on the balls of her feet. She pressed her hands to the walls for stability and felt the rotting wood sag under the pressure.

Then, at the top, was the hallway she remembered so well. To the right was a row of doors. To the left, a wall filled with windows. At its end stood a heavy door made of gray wood that they were not allowed through.

When she had been a child, gauzy curtains had framed the windows. They had been old even back then—relics from the wealthy family who had once lived in the building. The thin material billowed in even the lightest breeze, flowing across the narrow hallway and obscuring the door at its end. Some nights, when Leanne was forced to leave the safety of her bed to seek out a bathroom, she had thought she could see Patience standing in front of the door. Back straight, her dark dress blending into the gray wood behind. All that had been visible through the twisting curtains were her pallid face and milky eyes.

Leanne pointed her flashlight along the hall's length. The curtains were in scraps. Weathered threads still hung from the rods and spiraled in the disturbed air, but more of them lay across the floor, a layer of moth-eaten, decayed fabric that almost looked like soot.

The windows were open, just like they had always been during Leanne's stay there. Night air came through, warming the hall and helping fight off the chill that permeated the building. Leanne angled her flashlight toward the gray door. She remembered it being imposing, larger than any other door in Bellamy. Thick, a deep, worn gray, the door was one part of the house that hadn't changed with an adult's perspective. The dread in her stomach solidified at the sight of the barrier.

Her bedroom had been two doors along. Leanne stepped over the rotted fabric, feeling stiff threads crumble from the first disturbance in decades. She reached her door and let her fingertips graze the surface. It was discolored around the edge, caused by sweat from dozens of little hands pulling the wood open and shut multiple times a day. The doors did not have handles or locks. She pushed on the wood and let it fall open.

Eight beds had been fit into the small area inside. Children's size. The mattresses, quilts, and pillows were all decayed, rotting through the frame. Too much moisture had come through the open windows, Leanne supposed.

She recognized her own bed. She'd been lucky enough to have one under the window. On nights she couldn't sleep, she'd risen onto her knees and watched the mist drift through the trees below.

A toy rested beside the pillow: a small, brown, hand-stitched bear. Leanne didn't recognize it. Once she had left, another girl had come to take her place, just as always happened in Bellamy.

"Leanne."

She'd been staring though the window, lost in thought, waiting for her mind to quiet enough to let her sleep. At Henry's voice, she lowered herself back to her knees and turned to face him.

He lay in the bed to her left, his hands folded under the pillow for warmth, his brown hair messy. His eyes glittered in the wash of moonlight.

"What?" she whispered back. They weren't supposed to talk after bedtime. She glanced toward the doorway, half expecting to hear the thuds of Patience's cane.

"I can't sleep," Henry said.

She didn't know what he expected her to do about that when she couldn't sleep, either. "Try to count sheep." It hadn't worked for her, but it might for him. Around them, the other six children breathed slowly and deeply, absorbed in their dreams.

Henry shuffled closer to the bed's edge and lowered his voice even further. "Mike told me something earlier."

"What?"

"He said Patience sometimes wakes children in the middle of the night. He said if they go with her, they don't come back. He said it happened to Margo last night."

Margo slept in one of the other bedrooms. Leanne squinted through the shadows, trying to read Henry's expression. She was sure he was trying to scare her.

But, suddenly, she realized she didn't remember whether Margo had been at breakfast that morning. And she hadn't been in the kitchens, preparing lunch, or in the yard as they played in the evening.

Gooseflesh rose over her arms. Leanne licked her lips, trying to find something to say. Henry wasn't teasing her, she realized. He was looking for comfort. He was afraid.

"We'll be all right," she whispered. "We can look after each other, okay? I won't leave you."

Leanne turned toward the bed Henry had slept in. Her throat tightened. Burning tears, growing quickly, spilled over her lower lids. She closed her eyes and took ragged breaths, waiting for the thundering of her heart to fade.

The dreams came most nights. Henry sat alone in a dark

room, his face pale and his eyes wide. He reached toward her. His voice was slow and distorted as he called to her. "Why did you leave me, Leanne?"

Years of counseling. Bottles of sedatives. Meditation. Cognitive behavioral therapy. Hypnosis. Antidepressants. Nothing could stop them. Nearly every night, she saw him, calling to her, begging her not to leave.

Thirty years should have been enough to forget. She had forgotten everything else—the house's layout, the children's names, even the steady thud of Patience's cane. It had taken this pilgrimage to bring all of that back. But she had not forgotten Henry or that she had left him to the house.

Leanne folded her arms across her chest and took a deep breath. She turned slowly, surrounded by darkness, as the memory of Henry's last night resurfaced. It had been eight months since their arrival at Bellamy. Of the six other children in their room, five had disappeared and been replaced.

Sleep evaded Leanne, as it often did. Facing the ceiling, hands laced over her stomach, she let her gaze trace the familiar patterns in the plaster above. She was physically exhausted, but her mind wouldn't stop moving.

She heard it. The creak of a door. Not one of the bedrooms. She had lived there long enough to be familiar with how they sounded. No, it was the gray door, the massive slab at the end of the hall, grinding open.

The cane began to beat its path along the hallway. The heavy, rhythmic thumping was accompanied by the muffled scrape of Patience's steps. Drawing closer.

Leanne held still, not even trusting herself to breathe. It wasn't uncommon for Patience to roam the house late at night. As long as Leanne stayed quiet, Patience would pass their bedroom, and the cane would echo through the halls below for hours.

In the bed to her left, Henry moved. He rolled over then sat up, rubbing his palm across his eyes as he stared at the door. Leanne wanted to tell him to lie back down, to fake sleep like she did, but she couldn't risk making noise when Patience was so close.

The cane stopped right outside their door. A lump grew in Leanne's throat. She couldn't see the door from where she lay, but she could see Henry, his eyes fogged with sleep and his mouth slack. He stared at the door, unflinching, as it creaked open. Then he pushed his blankets aside and lowered his feet over the edge of the bed.

"No," Leanne hissed.

Henry didn't respond. Instead, he dropped to the floor, his bare feet nearly silent as they hit the wood. He disappeared from her sphere of view as he walked toward the door. A second later, the cane's rhythmic tapping returned. It led away, back along the hallway, toward the gray door. Heavy. Thumping. The beats matched her pulse. And then the gray door ground closed.

Terror's thrall broke. Leanne bolted upright, her heart thundering, one arm stretched out.

The bedroom door was closed. Pale sunlight came through the window. Bodies began to stir around her as the children woke. A boy in the room's corner stretched then rolled to his other side.

It had been a nightmare. Leanne's body was covered in cold sweat, nausea sticking in her throat. But it had just been a dream.

She turned to check on Henry. His bed was empty. The panic redoubled. Leanne leaped up and ran for the door, bumping into the crowded cots as she passed them.

The curtains swirled through the hall as a chilled early-morning breeze blew through the windows. Leanne looked to her right, toward the gray door. It was closed. She did not have the key for it. She turned left and ran for the bathroom. Sometimes Henry woke earlier than her and left to have the first bath. She beat on the doors, calling his name, but there was no answer.

Leanne ran for the stairs. Her breaths were shallow and painful, her head buzzing, her feet turning numb from the chilled floor. She raced through the building, looking for Henry in all of his favorite haunts, but they were empty. She became lost. Eight months had been long enough to become familiar with the house but not long enough to understand it.

She caught the quiet murmur of voices. Leanne slowed to a quiet walk, her lungs aching and heart knocking on her ribs. The voices came from one of the small rooms tucked into the back corners of the house. The door was open a fraction. Leanne approached it, moving silently, and put her eye to the crack.

Grace sat at a desk. She leaned over the wood, one pale arm holding her up, head drooping and golden hair hanging in limp strands around her damp face. Patience loomed over her. The older woman had put her cane aside as she carried a small china teacup. Leanne saw her lips twitch as she spoke, but she didn't hear any words. Patience placed the teacup on the desk at Grace's side then straightened and turned sharply. Her milky eyes pierced through the gap in the door.

Leanne jolted backward, out of sight. She couldn't run; her footsteps would give her away. But Patience would catch her if she stayed where she was.

Two wardrobes stood against the wall. The gap between them was just barely wide enough for a body to hide in. Shivers ran through Leanne as she squeezed into the nook.

The door drifted open, and Patience emerged. The cane thudded into the wooden floor. Her body stayed still, but that impassive face turned, slowly, gradually, to stare toward the wardrobes. The eyes fixed on the shadows where Leanne hid. Leanne's heart faltered. Then Patience turned away, and the cane beat into the floor as she glided down the passageway and out of sight.

Leanne didn't trust in her luck, but she was too desperate to do anything else. She left her hiding space and darted forward to slip into the room. Grace stayed slumped over the desk but raised her head as Leanne entered.

"Oh, sweetheart, hello. It's a little early for you to be up, isn't it?"

Tears spilled over Leanne's cheeks. She ran forward, arms outstretched, and Grace accepted the hug, pulling Leanne against herself and kissing the top of her head. Even clammy, even shaking, she still felt warm and good.

"She took Henry," Leanne gasped. "Patience took him last night. He's gone."

"What?" Grace ran her hand over the back of Leanne's head, her eyes tight with concern. "Sweetheart, what did you say?"

"Patience takes children. And they don't come back." She was almost unintelligible through the tears, but she charged onward, the words spilling out of her. "Last night, she took Henry. I saw him follow her. They went through the gray door at the end of the hall. You have to do something."

"I will, sweetheart, I will." Grace tried to say something else but then turned aside. Raw coughs shook her. She covered her mouth with her sleeve, and when she took it away, the fabric was flecked with red spots. Grace held still a moment, shaking, her hand gripping Leanne's shoulder almost painfully tightly. Then she drew a ragged breath. "I've heard you, my darling. I...I will find a way to fix this. I won't let you be separated from your brother. But, my dear, you must stay away from Patience for the rest of today."

"I will." Leanne didn't know what else to say. A noise encroached on the edge of her awareness. The tapping. It was growing louder. Patience was returning.

"Go," Grace whispered.

She stepped out of Grace's hug and ran for the door. As she left, in the second before she turned the corner and the room disappeared from sight, she saw Grace stretch a bone-thin hand toward the cup of tea.

Leanne rested her back against the bedroom wall and slid down to sit on the floor. She stretched her legs ahead of herself. Her nose and eyes burned as she wrapped her arms across her torso for a lonely hug.

Memories of that day came back in drips. She had not seen

Grace again. She had tried to find her, once, and worked her way back to the unfamiliar hallway. She had heard Grace coughing. Weak little gasps. Pained. Leanne had taken a step toward the door but stopped. At the other end of the hallway, swallowed in shadow, stood a figure. What thin light there was had glinted off the edge of the cane. Leanne had retreated.

Patience served their food that day. Leanne refused to approach the pot. She sat at the table with an empty plate, her heart aching, her throat burning, hyperaware of the empty seat beside her.

The children did their chores then filed upstairs to study. Grace did not hand out the workbooks, so the children retrieved the tomes themselves. Patience patrolled the hallway as she always did. Leanne stared at her book, the words swimming together, incomprehensible.

After dinner, which she refused to touch, the children were allowed outdoors. Leanne walked along the outside of the building, staring up at the windows, searching for any that had lights behind the curtains. Any signs of life inside. Any signs of Henry. She circled the building twice before the bell chimed.

She still had not seen Grace or Henry. But Grace had asked Leanne to trust her. So, Leanne had followed the other children to bed, as she was supposed to.

"Henry, what happened to you?"

Leanne ran her fingers across her jaw then took a sharp breath as she stood. She crossed the bedroom and reentered the hallway. The gray door stood to her right, the same as it had always been, as though it had been waiting for her all this time. She had almost gone through the door on that final night in Bellamy. Part of her wished she had.

Leanne knew she would not sleep that night. She sat on the edge of her bed while the other children dreamed around her. Only Henry's bed was empty. She tried to count the minutes as they passed. Moonlight crossed the ceiling above her in a slow arc. She guessed it was after midnight when the gray door creaked open.

She heard the cane, beating on the hallway floor, and she knew Patience was coming for her. Terror choked her, building like a suffocating lump in her throat. She knew, in the depths of her heart, if the woman took her, she would not be coming back.

And so she ran. Leaving with nothing except the pajamas on her back, she launched herself off her bed and bolted for the door. She squeezed her eyes shut as she pushed through, not wanting to meet the white-filmed eyes on the other side.

The cane tapped down a final time. Clawlike fingers snagged at her hair, but they were a second too slow, and she slipped through. Leanne ran, ricocheting down stairs, hitting the walls and stumbling in the dark.

When the children came inside at night, it only took a minute to climb to their rooms from the foyer. But retracing the path, Leanne couldn't find its end. She encountered an intersection she didn't recognize. She guessed her direction blindly. The hallway turned at an odd angle, then the one after that listed to the side, seemingly trying to tumble her deeper into the building. The cane echoed around her, above and below, thumping like a drum.

Then the squeezing walls opened up. Her reckless dash had carried her back to Bellamy's entrance. The huge doors stood ahead. She ran for them, arms outstretched, and burst through them and into the warm night.

Leanne faced the gray door at the end of the hallway. On that night, as she ran from Bellamy, she had believed it was her only choice. Even now, she didn't know what else she could have expected of herself.

But the dreams told her differently. Henry, crying, arms outstretched, asked why she had left him. And the guilt threatened to crumple her.

Leanne leaned forward, and her forehead touched the cool wood as a moan slipped past dry lips.

Her life had been better than it might have. She'd arrived in town the morning after escaping Bellamy, her feet scratched up from the run, exhausted and dizzy from hunger. A woman had found her, brought her into her home, and fed her. The police arrived. Everyone asked her questions. Where had she come from? Where were her parents?

She hadn't told them about Bellamy, Patience, Henry, or any of the other missing children. The memories hurt. She wanted to forget.

Leanne had been placed in a foster home. Her new family was kind. She had grown older and gotten a job then a home of her own. Now, thirty years later, people would say she had a good life. But she could not escape the feeling that it had come at the cost of Henry's.

"I'm so sorry." She spoke to the door as though he could hear her. As though returning thirty years late might somehow make good on the promise that she wouldn't leave him.

A soft tapping noise came from the other side of the door. Leanne took a sharp breath and opened her eyes. The steady thud of a cane echoed, so faint that it could have been coming from the back of Leanne's mind.

Her tongue was dry. She pressed it to the roof of her mouth to keep it silent.

Patience was gone. She had been old when Leanne was a child. She could not still be walking Bellamy's halls.

The cane fell silent. Leanne held her breath, listening. The silence was harsh. Almost painful. Her ears strained, reaching for anything, even the smallest hint of life—

The door banged as something hit it. The thick wood shivered under the impact, sending tremors through Leanne's body. She stepped back, separating herself from it, her heart strained to breaking. Her ears rang from the noise.

"Hello?"

She didn't expect an answer, and she didn't receive one. Leanne worked her jaw, feeling the perspiration stick her shirt to her back, even as each stuttering breath created a plume of condensation in the cool air.

There was something wrong with Bellamy. She had been running from it for most of her life. It had brought her home, though. Perhaps it had always intended to. Perhaps no one ever truly escaped the building.

She reached out and touched the door's handle. It had been kept locked when she was a child. Now, though, it turned under light pressure. Everything else in Bellamy was fused and stiff from age but not this door. It was as smooth as if it were brand-new.

No more running. No more hiding.

She pushed on the door and stepped through.

The room was unnaturally dark. The door behind her should have allowed light in, but as Leanne stepped over the threshold, the glow faded into nothing.

Leanne gasped as the cold hit her. It was painful in its intensity, scorching her throat and her lungs. Colder than the building could possibly be on a balmy night.

Hinges creaked. Leanne turned and reached her hand out to hold the door open, but she was too slow. The door slammed, and Leanne flinched.

She took the flashlight out of her pocket. As she fumbled for the switch, she squinted into the gloom. There was something ahead of her. She didn't know how she could tell when it was too dark to see, but she could *feel* the presence. A figure, standing just out of arms' reach, watching her.

Leanne's breath hitched as she found the flashlight's button. She felt the rubber indent under her finger, but there was no click and no light. She pressed the button again, then once more, then began mashing it desperately.

The battery hadn't died. It couldn't have. She'd replaced it that morning. And even if it had, she should have still heard the click of the button.

An unsettling sensation wrapped around her, squeezing her. She had the striking idea that the room was absorbing both noise and light. Syphoning them away and robbing her of her senses.

The figure ahead moved. There was a hiss, and the cold and dark were pierced by a small light.

Leanne watched the infant flame dance on the candle's wick. It seemed horribly fragile, like it was ready to collapse and die at any second, but as it grew, it lit the figure holding it.

Blue eyes. Wisps of fine golden hair floating around her pale face. Rose-pink lips smiling. "My sweetheart," Grace whispered. "You came back."

Leanne dropped the flashlight. It made no sound as it hit the floor, but she barely noticed. Throat tight, eyes burning, she reached toward Grace.

Grace's smile widened, and tears spilled down her cheeks. She took Leanne's hands and pulled her into a hug, her gentle fingers stroking Leanne's hair back from her forehead. The relief was almost achingly sweet, like being reunited with a close friend. The fear and sadness vanished, and for the first time in a long while, she felt like she had found home.

"How—" She pulled back far enough to see Grace's face. The tear tracks sparkled in the candlelight, but she was smiling. "How are you still—"

The words hung, unspoken: *How are you still alive?*

Grace hadn't aged. Thirty years should have dulled her hair into gray and creased her skin with wrinkles, but she stayed as young and delicate as Leanne remembered her.

The question died on Leanne's lips as she realized it didn't matter. Grace was here, and she was not just smiling but laughing from joy as she caressed Leanne's head. "Oh, my sweet girl, I'm so happy. You came back. I had always hoped you would."

Leanne felt like a child again—small, frightened, and hopeful, in a way she hadn't in decades. She held Grace's hand and squeezed the gentle fingers to reassure herself that they were real. "Have you been here this whole time?"

"Of course I have, sweetheart." Grace squeezed back. "I wouldn't leave my children."

Something moved in the darkness. The candlelight washed over Leanne and Grace, but it barely touched the rest of the room. Leanne squinted, trying to make out the shapes writhing through the black.

Children stepped forward, boys in shirts and shorts, girls in dresses. As young as four, as old as twelve, they clustered around Grace and Leanne, encircling them. But there were no smiles or laughter.

Leanne's heart turned cold. The overwhelming joy faded. She turned slowly, searching the faces around her.

They stood, shoulder to shoulder, rows deep. Their features were emotionless. Their arms hung limply at their sides. None of them moved or made any noise. Their eyes were glazed with

227

a sheen of white. Like blind eyes, except they were fixed on her, unblinking, intent.

"What is this?"

Leanne tried to take her hand out of Grace's, but the woman clutched it harder. Her smile quivered, and for the first time, Leanne thought she saw a hint of eagerness in it.

"Don't be frightened, my darling. I've been caring for them. They are warm and well loved here."

Leanne recognized faces from the crowd. Jayne, the girl who had disappeared into the forest. Paul, who had been called away from his desk. James. Millie. Hanna. Andrew.

But there were other faces, too. Faces she didn't recognize. Faces from before her time. Older styles of clothes, pinched features, blank eyes.

And then she found him. Henry. Wearing the pajamas from the night he'd disappeared, he looked exactly the way she saw him in her dreams. Except, in the dreams, he cried and called to her. Now, he was silent. Unresponsive. There was no flicker of recognition under the white-covered eyes.

"You must understand." Grace rubbed Leanne's hand. A comforting touch. "I did this for them."

"You did this?" The words sounded foreign, like they were coming from someone else.

"I had to. My poor babies—my darlings. You had lost your families. There was no one left to love you. What was I supposed to do? Force you back out into a world that didn't want you?"

Grace's fingers were warm, but the rest of Leanne was horribly cold. She kept turning, staring into the blank faces clustered around her. There were so many of them.

"I could not have children of my own, but I could save the ones that had been entrusted to me. And so I did. I brought them over, one at a time."

"Brought them over?"

"Into the second realm." Grace's voice was soft, so quiet that it almost dissolved into the air. "The step beyond. I am a guide. There are not many of us left."

The children stared at her, unspeaking and unmoving. They were nothing more than dolls.

"It hurt me. It made me tired and weak, and so I could only carry over one or two a week. But I did my best. It was a small cost to make sure you would be safe here with me, in a world that can't hurt you, where you will never feel pain, where you will never feel another moment of sadness."

She remembered Grace coughing and shaking, perspiration dotting her forehead. The illness had gotten worse in batches. Always following when one of the children had disappeared.

"You were so frightened when your brother went first," Grace whispered. She had moved closer without Leanne realizing. They stood side by side, so close that Leanne could feel Grace's breath on her cheek. "I was weak, and my mother's tea could only help so much, but I was still going to try. To bring you over the follow-ing night. So that you wouldn't have to be without him again. But you ran. Sweetheart, why did you run? Why did you leave?"

The children around her abruptly moved. Their mouths

opened, and they spoke, one voice coming from a hundred different directions. "Why did you leave?"

Leanne shook her head. Tears slipped down her cheeks.

"Shh, my darling." Grace brushed her fingers across Leanne's forehead, pushing her hair back. When her fingers touched Leanne's skin, the fear and horror bled away, vanishing, as though it had been pulled out of her. In its place, a calm descended. The memories began to fade, losing impact, like a nightmare seeping away in the hours after waking. Jayne, disappeared into the forest. Paul, called out of his seat. Henry, stepping out of bed and approaching the open bedroom door. As that final memory began to fade, a part of Leanne wanted to let it go. It was painful, and releasing it would be a relief.

But she didn't. She held on to the image, clutching it tightly, not letting it be pulled away from her for a second time. It hurt to keep it, but that pain was what she needed.

The thrall broke. The comfort that had descended over her fled, replaced by the fear and cold once again. She stepped back, yanking her hand out of Grace's. "You killed them."

The blue eyes widened. "Sweetheart—"

"You don't know my name, do you?" It had always been *sweetheart*, or *darling*, or any one of a dozen other doting titles. That was all any of them had been called. "You went through so many children that you don't remember *any* of their names."

Grace still held the candle, and the flame shimmered as her hands trembled. "You were so much nicer as a child."

"What is this place?" Leanne took another step back. The wall of children parted, moving away so she would not bump into any of them, but their eyes didn't leave her. She had never been able to find out much about Bellamy online. At the time, Leanne had believed the asylum had been too small for many people to remember it. Now, she suspected otherwise. "Was this even a real institute? There were never any inspections. Never any families visiting. Did anyone know about Bellamy except the people who lived here?"

"No." Her tiny smile showed white teeth. "Our home was a secret. We were safe here, where we could not be disturbed."

"Where did the children come from?"

"I called." Grace's eyes glimmered in the soft light. "I called out to lost and lonely children, and you came. Walking through the forest. Arriving at the front gate, where I could take you in and protect you until you were ready to step over."

Leanne blinked. She tried to remember a time before Bellamy. Where had she lived? What had her family been like? She had always believed she and Henry were orphans, but was that even the truth? She remembered being new at Bellamy. She remembered crying on her first night. Being found by Grace. Having her hair stroked. Feeling calmer. But nothing before.

Grace reached toward her. Leanne stepped out of reach and felt the children shuffle out of her way. She didn't dare let the woman touch her again. Too much was taken away each time.

"Sweetheart." Grace shook her head. "Don't be so petulant, now. Give me your hand. I can make this right. I can bring you over. You want to be with your brother, don't you? I'll make it so that you never have to leave him again."

Henry stepped through the crowd. His movements weren't entirely natural. They were a fraction too slow and a fraction too jerky to look right. He came to a halt beside Grace. Leanne met his eyes—white, dead eyes—and felt her heart break.

Grace moved forward abruptly, trying to snatch up Leanne's hand. She stumbled back, breathing heavily, holding her arms close to her body so they couldn't be caught.

"I want to leave." Leanne chanced a look over her shoulder. The room shouldn't have been large, but she had been backing up for meters and still couldn't see the door.

"You are being difficult, my darling. But I want you to know that it's all right. Nothing you do will dull my love."

"I don't *want* your love."

For a moment, they were both silent, staring at each other across the expanse of black. Then Grace tilted her head to one side. "I am being patient with you, but you know, we are not alone here. My mother stayed with me as well. She takes care of the naughty children." Grace smiled. "You *are* being quite naughty, aren't you, my dear?"

A thud echoed through the dark. Cold washed through Leanne's limbs, turning them heavy. The children scattered. They disappeared into the darkness, their footsteps making no more noise than Leanne's own thumping heart.

She met Grace's eyes. The woman's smile, a little too large to be reassuring, glimmered in the candlelight. Then the cane hit the floor again, and the candle's flame died.

The world was black. Leanne, afraid of touching and of being touched, held her hands close to her chest. Her breath was raspy in her ears. Her legs shook. She turned her head, searching for light, searching for an escape.

The cane impacted the ground again. It was growing faster. *Closer.* Leanne tried to back away from it, but she couldn't tell which direction it came from.

Thud.

"No." Leanne tried to run. She took two steps before fear brought her to a halt. It was closer. Almost on her. She pressed her hands to her face, a child again, afraid to see.

Thud.

Right behind her. She couldn't move. Couldn't breathe.

Thud.

A hand gripped her shoulder. Heavy, clawlike fingers dug into her. Leanne screamed.

Candles flickered to life. Dozens of them were spaced about the room. They lit a wooden floor. They lit the backs of cowering children, huddled in clumps around the room's corners, their heads bowed as they tried to avoid notice. And they lit the woman behind Leanne.

Patience towered over her. The milky-white eyes stared into her, boring into her soul. They sat in a pale face, emotionless, unmoving, crowned with black hair. Her dress made no noise as she moved. The only sound that came from her was the heavy wooden cane clutched in her bony hand. She lifted it and let it drop. The sound seemed to run through Leanne, coursing along her bones like shivers.

I am so afraid of you. But why? Slowly, heart thundering, Leanne forced herself to look up, to raise her gaze over Patience's thin lips, over her sharp nose and colorless cheeks, to meet those milky eyes. "Why am I afraid of you?"

"I hope she dies soon," Leanne whispered.

Henry giggled, bowed over his bowl of stew. Across the table from them, Patience paced, circling the room with steady, measured steps.

At Leanne's words, the eyes swiveled toward her. The pupils stared through the sheen. Leanne's heart faltered. She lowered her head, trying to escape those horrible eyes, her throat tight and her stomach squirming. Patience couldn't have heard. She'd been careful to keep her voice soft. And yet, the clicking noise was moving closer, louder, and she could still feel the eyes on her, unblinking...

The cane thudded a final time on the stones behind Leanne's chair. She was frozen, terrified, head down, one hand clutching her empty spoon. The hand touched her shoulder. Heavy and cold. Patience bent down, close to her head, so that her wheezing breaths swirled across Leanne's ear.

"I have been dead for a very long time," the woman whispered.

Leanne took a shuddering breath. The memory had been lost for decades, but it rushed back, sharp and fresh. Leanne raised her own hand and cautiously rested it on top of Patience's.

She was hiding in the cupboard, nestled between old blankets and the wooden wall. She hadn't heard the warning signal that the game of hide-and-seek was over. She hadn't known Patience was home. And the cane tapped on the hallway floor, growing closer. Louder. Matching the beating of Leanne's heart.

A shadow moved across the gap at the base of the floor. The cane tapped for a final time, loud enough to echo. The silence was agony.

Leanne raised her second hand to cover her mouth. She was cold all of a sudden. So desperately cold that she wanted to gasp. She closed her eyes, squeezing them, as though she could escape Patience in the black inside her head.

The cupboard's handle rattled. Leanne shook her head once, begging someone to save her, begging heaven to pull Patience away from her hiding hole. The latch clicked. The door drew open, slow and ponderous. Leanne was forced to open her eyes.

Patience stood above her. The woman's frame filled the entire doorway. The white eyes bore into her as Patience bent at her waist, and the stiff lips twitched. "Run to your friends. Quickly. Do not let her find you alone, or she will take you."

Leanne met Patience's eyes, and for the first time, she wasn't afraid. The milk-clouded irises weren't cruel. They were sad. Heavy with decades of grief.

Leanne tightened her fingers over Patience's. "Why do you stay with her?"

The woman's expression changed for the first time Leanne had seen. The brows pulled together. Her raspy, dry voice wavered. "I have no choice. She has bound me to her will."

Leanne stepped closer. She could smell a musty scent of dust and ages-old decay on the black silk dress. She dropped her voice into a whisper. "What do I have to do?"

Patience's cheek touched hers. The words, expelled as an exhale, ran through Leanne. "Do not give her control. *Fight.*"

"My darling." Grace's voice rang through the cold air.

Leanne turned. Grace stood inside a ring of candles. She held a piece of chalk, the same kind she had always used for their lessons, between her fingers. Her smile was full of gentleness and love, but now, the sight of it left Leanne cold. Grace closed her fist around the chalk, and when she opened it, the substance had been crushed into a powder. "We are ready, my darling."

She scattered the chalk across the floor. It didn't fall in the usual chaotic cloud. Instead, it funneled into a line as it descended. It touched the floor, creating a circle. Intricate words ran along the border.

"Bring her, Mother."

Patience's hand tightened on Leanne's shoulder. She pushed, and Leanne gasped as she staggered forward. She tried to back up, to squirm away, but the clawlike grip was inescapable.

The children were moving. They flowed in from the room's perimeter, weaving between the candles, clustering around them. Hundreds of blank eyes fixed on Leanne.

Grace reached out as they neared. Leanne made a final bid for freedom, trying to drop and twist in the same motion. Patience was old, but she had an inhuman strength. Leanne was wrenched back toward Grace, and when Leanne caught a glimpse of Patience's face, she thought she saw guilt etched into the expression.

Then Grace had her hands, and the whole world fell still. Fear and anger vanished at the touch. A soft contentment seeped in to take its place. Patience let go of Leanne's shoulder, and Grace gently tugged her forward to stand inside the circle.

"There, now, sweetheart." She brushed sweaty hair away from Leanne's forehead. "We are almost there. Just be still and trust me."

No. Fight.

The words ran through Leanne's mind without her understanding them. They felt important. But she was calm, and she was happy. Henry stood not far behind Grace, his face seeming gray in the candlelight. He wasn't smiling, but he was still happy, wasn't he?

Wasn't he…?

No. This time, the words hit her hard enough to hurt. *Fight.*

Leanne tried to step back. Grace's hold on her tightened. The skin was turning red around her wrists where the woman pinched her.

Fight.

"Almost there." Grace's pretty blue eyes exuded comfort. The sensation was washing out of her like waves, tangible and heavy, trying to drag Leanne down. It was physically painful to reject it. But she did.

She closed her heart, refusing the emotions that were being forced onto her. And she clutched on to the memories.

Children, disappearing.

Grace wiping away the fear with a touch.

Patience whispering, "I have been dead for a very long time."

Henry, taken in the middle of the night, while she lay paralyzed and helpless to stop him.

Leanne sucked in a sharp breath as she escaped the thrall. And, in an instant, the woman ahead of her changed.

She was still recognizable as Grace. But not the Grace Leanne had thought she'd known. The woman ahead of her was twisted and deformed. Her limbs were skeleton thin. The skin was papery and wrinkled. Her face looked more like a skull than anything else. Round eyes, vicious red behind the sheen of white, bulged out of the sockets above bony cheeks and a lipless mouth. The golden hair was gone, leaving the skin on her head bald and creased.

I always said she looked like a fairy. Maybe I saw more than I thought.

"Come, my darling." The words had lost their melodic tone. They were rasping, inhuman, and shrill. "We are nearly there."

Leanne felt herself being pulled. She was listing forward, tipping, about to fall into the circle that had been drawn beneath her feet. It would be the easiest thing in the world to let the bony hands drag her down.

She pulled back, fighting with everything inside of her. Leanne clutched at the memories that had been taken from her as she stared into the monstrous face. Using the fear, anger, and pain to fuel herself, she resisted the pull.

Grace's face twitched. A whine escaped her throat. The candles around them guttered in the still air.

Carrying children over exhausted her. She became weak and sick. And those children…they were willing. They loved her, and they wanted to please her. She made sure of that. Just like she made sure they were afraid of Patience, so that they would never go to her for help.

No one had resisted Grace before. And it was breaking her

apart. A line of blood ran from the edge of her lipless mouth. It pooled in her bulging eyes. The skin on her forehead was breaking and splitting, as a deep, anguished moan rose from her throat.

Leanne struggled harder. The memories ran through her head as bright and clear as lamps on a dark night. The pull was intense, like a tide wanting to drag her out into the ocean, but she held fast, despite the growing exhaustion.

For Henry. For Ann and Jayne and Paul and Andrew and every other soul you took for your twisted collection.

Grace's head snapped back. The red eyes stared toward the ceiling, wild with pain and fear. The lips moved, forming a single word: "No." Then her form twisted, writhing, crumpling in on itself. Like a piece of paper set alight with invisible flames, it tumbled down, contracting and withering into the circle on the floor. The hands were the last to go, clinging to Leanne's wrists even after their own arms became soot. Even in death, she wasn't willing to give up.

The grip was released. The candles went out, plunging the room back into darkness. Leanne dropped to her knees, gasping and shaking, her heart broken into a hundred pieces.

She didn't know how much time had passed, only that her throat was dry and her head pounded. Every muscle ached. Leanne crawled onto her hands and knees, gasping from the effort.

The room was still dark, but it felt less oppressive than it had before. Her eyes, acclimatized, fought to pick out shapes. There

DARCY COATES

was something small and metallic on the floor just a few feet away. She crawled to it and felt her hand close around her flashlight.

This time, when she pressed the button, the light flickered on. Leanne lifted it.

Dozens of pale faces stared back at her, each with a set of milky eyes. The children. They seemed dazed, but their expressions were no longer empty. They blinked and looked around themselves. Leanne turned her light across the group, searching for Henry, but instead, she found Patience.

The woman looked older than Leanne remembered. She bowed further over her cane, and every movement seemed pained. Her lips lifted into a smile.

Leanne climbed to her feet. Her legs ached, and she felt like she was going to be sick. "What…what now?"

No one answered. They all looked at her, waiting for her lead.

She was desperately thirsty. She had water in her car. Slowly, she turned toward the door and fumbled with the handle to let herself out.

The hallway had changed. The wooden floor was crumbling. The walls were stained. The windows were all broken, leaving shards of glass across the floor. *It was an illusion. She kept the house looking whole.*

Leanne glanced inside the bedrooms as she passed them and saw empty metal bed frames. She wondered if the asylum had even been whole during her stay there. Some of the damage looked older than thirty years.

Plants had grown across the staircase and climbed through

240

holes in the wall. Water dripped from the ceiling. One of the stairs fractured as Leanne tried to climb down, but she was too tired to find another route out.

As she reached the base of the stairs, she glanced back. A procession followed her. Patience led the way for a stream of children. Leanne wanted to tell them she didn't know what she was doing and not to follow her, but her mouth was too dry.

She continued along the hallway. It was still narrow, but when it turned, the corner was straight, the way it should be. Down another flight of stairs, her legs threatening to give way with every step, then Leanne pushed past a rotting door and stepped into the foyer.

Ahead, the decayed front door stood ajar. Dawn's light poured through. She had spent the whole night inside Bellamy. As she moved toward the door, she heard the cane clicking on the old stone behind her. It was softer than it had been. Muffled, more like a dream than a real noise.

Leanne stepped through the door and stopped on the front porch. She took a deep breath and felt her lungs ache with the first taste of clean air in hours.

Patience came to a halt at her side. Leanne felt ashamed to meet the older woman's face. There was so much she needed to apologize for—the way she'd spoken about Patience and how she'd hated her. But when she looked at the woman's face, there was no resentment. Just relief. She smiled at Leanne, and the smile looked as tired as Leanne felt.

One of the boys stepped through the door. As he moved into

the sunlight, his body began to dissolve. It faded, breaking into fragments. The fragments became dust that swirled upward, snatched away by the breeze.

Leanne gasped and reached a hand out to stop him, but he was gone before she could move. A girl followed him. Leanne snatched at her dress and, for a second, felt the material. It was strangely cold and thin, like spiderwebs. Then the fabric disappeared between her fingers as the girl evaporated.

More children came out, and Leanne realized there was excitement on their faces. They were racing outside, reaching toward the sun, their eyes closing and their features relaxing as they faded.

Leanne looked toward Patience, asking a silent question. The older woman gave a small nod. This was right.

The children poured out of Bellamy and tasted sunlight for the first time in decades. Leanne leaned against the wall and watched them go. Some skipped. Some leaped through the doorway. Most raised their hands toward the sky as they were snatched up.

Finally, the flow slowed. A final child stepped outdoors. A boy, painfully familiar. Henry smiled up at Leanne. He reached out for her hand, and she reached back. Their fingers touched, but all Leanne could feel was a sense of cold. Henry grinned at her as he stepped away, his hand separating from hers, and then he was gone.

With her wards released, Patience finally moved forward. She nodded to Leanne as she passed, and her mouth formed the phrase *Thank you*. As the sunlight touched her dress, the fabric shriveled and evaporated, just like the children. She closed her eyes and turned her face skyward, and in a heartbeat, Leanne was alone.

The wooden cane hit the stone steps with a clatter. Leanne rubbed a hand over her face then bent to pick up the cane. She used it to keep her balance as she walked across the field and toward her car. She placed the cane in the passenger seat then exhaled as she settled behind the wheel. She felt a thousand years old, but the car turned on at the twist of the key, and she spun the wheel to turn back toward the road.

The nightmares wouldn't haunt her any longer, she knew. Bellamy would no longer call to her…or any other child. As the trees closed in behind her, hiding the old building from sight, she gave it a final parting look in her rearview mirror. It was nothing but a ruin, forgotten by everyone save Leanne.

She met her own eyes. They had always been hazel. To her surprise, she found she didn't mind that the brown had been washed over with a sheen of white.

AUTHOR'S NOTE

Modern culture often boils mythical creatures down to forces of good. Unicorns are pure, mermaids are beautiful, and fairies are magical and charming.

But the original legends were often much more ominous. Fae were not necessarily evil, but they were dangerous. Entering a ring of mushrooms would trap you and, in some legends, force you to dance until you died of exhaustion. Fairies would steal babies and replace them with changelings, fairy offspring who would never be quite right.

While "Bellamy" isn't based in any one legend, it draws inspiration from them, especially their atmosphere. There are no clear answers, only a set of rules that are simultaneously complex, vague, and inescapable. No true evil, but a force that is selfish and single-minded. No heroes, just people who make mistakes and try desperately to right them.

ABOUT THE AUTHOR

Darcy Coates is the *USA Today* bestselling author of *Hunted*, *The Haunting of Ashburn House*, *Craven Manor*, and more than a dozen other horror and suspense titles. She lives on the Central Coast of Australia with her family, cats, and a garden full of herbs and vegetables. Darcy loves forests, especially old-growth forests where the trees dwarf anyone who steps between them. Wherever she lives, she tries to have a mountain range close by.

HUNTED

HER DISAPPEARANCE WASN'T AN ACCIDENT.
HER RESCUE WILL BE A MISTAKE.

Five days after twenty-two-year-old Eileen Hershberger went missing on a hike through the remote Ashlough Forest, her camera was discovered washed downriver, containing bizarre photos taken hours after her disappearance. But with no body and no additional clues, finding Eileen in the dark and winding woods seems next to impossible.

Chris wants to believe his sister is still alive. When the police search is abandoned, he and four of his friends vow to scour the mountain range until they find Eileen and bring her home. But as the small group strays farther from the trails and the unsettling discoveries mount, they begin to realize they're not alone...and Eileen's disappearance was no accident. But by then, it's already too late.

VOICES IN THE SNOW

NO ONE ESCAPES THE STILLNESS.

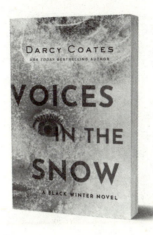

Clare remembers the cold. She remembers dark shapes in the snow and a terror she can't explain. And then...nothing. When she wakes in a stranger's home, he tells her she was in an accident. Clare wants to leave, but a vicious snowstorm has blanketed the world in white, and there's nothing she can do but wait.

They should be alone, but Clare's convinced something else is creeping about the surrounding woods, watching. Waiting. Between the claustrophobic storm and the inescapable sense of being hunted, Clare is on edge...and increasingly certain of one thing: her car crash wasn't an accident. Something is waiting for her to step outside the fragile safety of the house...something monstrous, something unfeeling. Something desperately hungry.

THE HOUSE NEXT DOOR

NO ONE STAYS HERE FOR LONG.

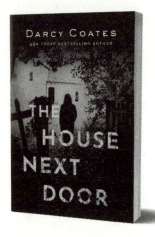

Josephine began to suspect something was wrong with the house next door when its family fled in the middle of the night, the children screaming, the mother crying. They never came back. No family stays at Marwick House for long. No life lingers beyond its blackened windows. No voices drift from its ancient halls. Once, Josephine swore she saw a woman's silhouette pacing through the upstairs room…but that's impossible. No one had been there in a long, long time.

But now someone new has moved next door, and Marwick House is slowly waking up. Torn between staying away and warning the new tenant, Josephine only knows that if she isn't careful, she may be its next victim…